THE FINGER OF SUSPICION

M.E.

SYLER

To Joy and Missy
all my love,
M. E. Syler
(Mark)

Dedication: To my wife and Children for their love and support

Acknowledgments: To my beta reader Kelly Casteel who provided me with honest feedback for this book, and many thanks to my editor, Paul Eder for his patient guidance.

Cover graphics by SelfPubBookCovers.com/thrillerauthor

ISBN 978-1534884366

CreateSpace Independent Publishing Platform

Table of Contents

Chapter 1

The humidity smacked my face when I opened the back door to start running. The questions had smacked me harder though. My mind kept replaying the visit from Detective Reynolds. He had treated me like a criminal! His questions! His raw attitude! I couldn't hide my anger.

Marilyn had been murdered, and they labeled me a suspect. A kind woman with a warm smile. Who would murder a woman like that? *Stupid question.* I had been in the game long enough to know that murder was not a product of sound reasoning. In my years as a Special Agent in the Army's Criminal Investigation Command, I had seen more than a few innocent souls murdered out of anger, jealousy, fear, or greed. I'd put away psychopaths with wacky goals who killed for pleasure. Now Reynolds had pigeonholed me as one of those wackjobs. *What possible motive could I have had?*

The questions burned. I ran hard, shouted to myself, and shook my head back and forth. Maybe I looked like a crazy man to anyone who saw me at that moment.

About a mile up the mountain path, sweat started rolling off my body like rain. I picked up speed. Seldom do I run twice a day, but I had the need to cleanse my mind and body. I knew it would take a clear mind to hunt down this killer. Retirement was on hold.

My pace slowed to a walk when I neared Angry Rock. I had named the monster rock formation on my first run up the mountain, the day after I moved to Winfield Creek. The six-foot high limestone stalwart butted over the edge of the ridge - two hundred feet down to the valley. There, I purged unclean emotions. I threw nightmares, flashbacks, and even daydreams over the edge. I scattered regrets, sorrows, and unfulfilled hopes to the wind. Standing on the rock, I stripped my running shorts and shirt. I let the breeze and smell of the natural world wash away the demons.

After redressing, I turned to climb down, but I noticed a slight movement in my periphery. You don't go through the training I had endured and not notice something like that. I continued to climb down without reacting to the presence. My pulse spiked, but I didn't let it show.

I walked a quarter mile and stooped down to pick a wildflower. With a furtive glance back, I picked up the tail a good distance behind me. I moved on. Looking up at the trees, I gave the appearance of taking a casual stroll in nature. Five minutes later, I turned to walk down another path that led to a dirt road. There I would be able to cut back along the slope and emerge within a few yards of my house.

I scolded myself. The visit from the police this morning had me so upset I left the 45 Commander on the secretary. I knew the best option was to get through this without a confrontation. My instincts urged me to double back and follow the tail. If the tail wasn't a cop, an old enemy might have surfaced.

Chapter 2

I had moved to this small town to keep a low profile and enjoy retirement. It had worked for the past couple of months, but it all changed when the Detective accused me of murder.

I had to talk to someone who is trustworthy and not judgmental. Charley Farber was my neighbor and a Deacon at Saint Mary's Parish. He knew everything about Winfield Creek and the residents. Charley ate brunch at The Grinder every Sunday morning after the first Mass. The Grinder was a small coffee shop located downtown, the aroma of fresh roasted coffee and homemade bread invited me inside. They roast the beans, grind coffee on the premises, and made bread from scratch. All of their meats and cheeses were locally sourced (*local* means anywhere in the state of Tennessee.)

As a habit (or a hobby), I liked to study the local history of the places where I lived. The owner of The Grinder was a descendant of Winfield Creek's founder, Timothy Lyle. He had built the first trading post and gristmill in the eighteen hundreds. The Grinder sat on the original foundation of the gristmill. Timothy had a good head for business, and the Lyle family had a successful mercantile trade up to the nineteen-thirties. At one time, the Lyles were the wealthiest family in this part of the country. Thomas Lyle III had owned and operated the last Lyle enterprise in Winfield Creek.

The Grinder walls were rough lumber decorated with pictures of the early settlers and lumberjacks in the East Tennessee Mountains. Timothy Lyle's muzzleloader was mounted on the stone fireplace, above the hand-carved mantle.

Charley sat at his favorite table. I didn't know if Charley even considered me a friend. Our relationship was stronger than vapid pleasantries. We had three things in common. We were the same age, we were both army veterans, and we both loved Elvis (not in a fanatical way). After declining his invitation to Mass, I expected him to move on to someone else. To his credit, he still tried to save my soul. Charley listened and talked without being a nuisance or judgmental. "Morning," I said.

Charley closed his book to greet me. "Morning, Robert. A pleasant surprise, sit down, please." I pulled out a chair and sat across from him. I led with my heavy news.

"The police think I killed Marilyn Todd."

"I know," Charley said. He picked up the cup, sipped his coffee.

"The police came to my house yesterday."

"I know that too. Everyone in town knows Sam Reynolds paid you a visit. There hasn't been a murder in this town since the thirties. Marilyn Todd had been beaten to death, and the killer is still on the loose. People are scared." We paused for the server.

"I'll have a double espresso, roast beef on rye with a slab of Limburger cheese," I ordered.

"How can you stomach that gross smelling cheese?"

"It's health food," I said. "Charley, I didn't kill her."

"Have you noticed that people are eyeballing you?"

"I noticed."

"These are good people, Robert. However, fear can make good people do bad things. You're an outsider, and most here think you're guilty as sin."

"We had a Friday night date," I explained. "I took her home and left. Reynolds got that information from a neighbor. Then he drilled me for an hour." I paused to see if he had any questions. "Afterward, I went up the mountain, and I was followed."

"Did you recognize the person?"

"A man but couldn't identify him."

"Maybe the police," Charley said.

"Could be and maybe not," I said.

"Those trails are used by a lot of folks. Could be someone out for a walk."

"No, the guy was experienced, Charley. I'm going to clear my name. I'm going to find the killer, and I'm going to set this right for Marilyn's reputation," I said. "But I need something from you—information. Nobody knows this town better than you do. Can you name the people who were close to Marilyn, anyone who knows about her life?" While Charley took the time to think it over my attention turned to the sandwich on the plate.

"Marilyn, as you know, was new in town, and she kept to herself. I made it a point to introduce myself and made her feel welcomed, like I did when you moved in, Robert." Charley paused again then said, "more than one neighbor had their eye on Marilyn, like Jessie, who lives next door to her."

On cue, a frail looking man appeared at the side of our table and said, "Deacon Charles."

"Hello Jessie," Charley replied. "This is Robert Snow." The old man turned his attention to me.

"I know who this is. Don't know much about you fella. I saw you with the Todd woman. Told the police that much." Jessie looked to be ninety. With the way he squinted when he talked, I wondered how the police even trusted what he saw.

"You saw me bring Marilyn home, after our dinner date; you must have seen me leave right after she went inside," I said.

"Don't reckon I did. On my way up to bed was when I saw you walk her up on the porch. The porch light on—," Jessie paused. He eyeballed me for a second. "You moved to Winfield Creek and next thing we have a murder. Don't sit well with folks around here. Can't understand why you're still walking around town like nothing happened." He spoke with a loud tone that sent a firm message.

"I assure you, sir; I had nothing to do with Marilyn's murder. If the police had evidence to contradict that, I would be sitting in jail." Jessie's cold stare didn't faze me, and then he turned to walk away.

"Excuse me Jessie; I'd like to know how you saw us on the porch?"

"I have one of those chairs that go up and down the stairs. Can't walk them anymore. A small window halfway up the staircase, low enough for me to see sitting down. Got a clear view of the sidewalk and the front porch. I saw you pull up to the curb. I stopped the chair and watched. You got out and opened the door for the woman. You looked like a gentleman. I saw you walk her up to the door. You two stood on the porch awhile. I got tired and went on up to bed."

With nothing else to say, and after making a scene, Jessie moved on to the register to pay his bill. I felt the eyes of suspicion staring at me. Charley put his hand on my arm to get my attention.

"Robert, don't put too much stock in Jessie. He's a loner and doesn't know any more than what he said. By tomorrow, he will forget he spoke to you. Thelma Burke's house is on the same block with Marilyn. She is an author. She's nosy and likes to talk, a lot. Word is she had a lot to say about you at the library last night."

"The library," I said. "Talking about me? I didn't know the library was open on Saturday nights."

"A local writer's guild meeting. Five members get together once a month to share their writing," Charley said. "Thelma comments on their work. She's the founder and President of the writing guild.

Thelma also writes a column in the local paper. She had called an emergency meeting. You were the main topic. Thelma carries weight; she is sort of a celebrity being a published author. She has the Mayor's ear. She uses that to her advantage whenever she can. Thelma got tempers flared up at the guild meeting. She had them all convinced you're guilty. They plan to go to the Mayor and demand she order Chief Bright to arrest you," Charley said.

"I'm flattered! I've been in tougher situations before and have made more than a few enemies in my life," I said. "Going back to what you said before-what did you mean more than one neighbor had their eye on Marilyn?"

"A young woman moved to the town without a husband. Neighbors looked out for her. They would visit. Drink tea, and other such things."

"Did you invite her to Mass, like you did me?"

"Sure, and unlike you, she came."

"Religion had never been a high priority, Charley. Were the neighbors looking out for her or just snooping?" I sniped.

"A little of both," Charley said.

"I apologize for my tone, Charley. Wasn't meant for you. Marilyn murdered right under everyones' noses. It seems to me if people were watching her they would have seen something out of the ordinary," I said.

"Some folks just like to gossip. At the same time, they don't want to get involved. Talk to Thelma she's observant and forthright. She will say if she saw anything unusual."

"You think Thelma will speak to me after plotting to have me arrested?"

"Yes. Like I said, she is nosy. She will not be able to resist the opportunity."

"Is Thelma a church woman?" I asked.

"First Baptist every Sunday morning and Wednesday evening," Charley replied.

"I will talk to her, but not before I gather more information. What kind of stuff does she write about?"

"Most of her work is crime fiction, but she has two nonfiction books that cover the Lyle murders. She is an expert on the Lyle family," Charley said.

"Timothy Lyle, the founder of Winfield Creek. And Thomas Lyle from the thirties," I interjected.

"That's right. You know Timothy died under mysterious circumstances. He and his wife were laid to rest in the small cemetery behind the Todd house," Charley said. "The plot of ground is the Lyle family cemetery. Timothy and Adsila Lyle were buried near the stone foundation of the trading post. There are several generations of the Lyle family buried in that cemetery. The last were Thomas Lyle III, his wife Mary Ellen, and their sons. Mary Ellen died giving birth to twin boys Zach and Kane."

"How Timothy died has been debated by many people," I added.

"You've done your homework," replied Charley.

I continued, "He went missing and was found after a couple of weeks on the slope of Siler's Bald. His head was bashed in and his spine was broken in two places."

Charley chimed in. "Some folks speculated he had a run in with a Cherokee. However, that was questionable. Given the relationship between the early Settlers and the Cherokee, they looked to use the Indians as scapegoats. His death occurred right in the middle of the Government's Indian Removal Act in 1838."

"The Trail of Tears," I said.

"Many of the Indians hid to avoid the Army round up."

"Timothy's wife was Cherokee, wasn't she?" I asked.

"That's right, and there were plenty of hard feelings towards him. Folks accused him of hiding Cherokee families. I'm not a detective, Robert, but it seems to me Timothy was killed by a white man."

"It doesn't take a detective to figure that out. It was likely more than one," I added.

"Not much has been written on Timothy's death, more was written on his life as the founder of Winfield Creek. In 1830, Timothy obtained fifty acres of land. He named it Winfield Creek and built his trading post, a small cabin, a year later he built the gristmill. Timothy was a pioneer who had a good sense for business. He made a good amount of money for the Lyle family. Nevertheless, beyond Timothy, the murders that Burke and a few other authors have written most about were Thomas Lyle and his two boys. The case also remained unsolved."

"I've read some about Thomas Lyle. Can you tell me what you know?" I asked.

"Thomas Lyle was a respected merchant in his own right. He owned and operated the Lyle General Store. Thomas married Mary Ellen Bickford, her family had moved to Winfield Creek from

Pennsylvania. Her father worked at the little River Lumber Company founded by Colonel Townsend.

"Thomas and Mary Ellen were married a little over a year when she died giving birth to the twin boys. Thomas's father-in-law discovered the dead bodies of Thomas and his two sons on the morning of July 3, 1930. Around 10:00 A.M. He went over to check on them when they hadn't opened the store. Thomas was a stickler for being on time. He opened every day, Monday through Saturday at 9:00 A.M. sharp.

"The bodies were found in their beds. Their heads were beaten to the point their faces were unrecognizable. The community was in shock, with no suspects and no evidence collected at the crime scene, not even the murder weapon recovered. A failed constable was blamed for botching the investigation. Some speculated a deliberate action to cover for the killer. A theory is that he protected a Lyle who did the deed. Some Constables, I presume were competent, but many people say this Constable granted favors for a price."

"This was back in 1930, and Constables were still the first police presence?" I asked.

"Winfield Creek didn't have a lot of crime. That murder was the catalyst for Winfield Creek to create a full-time police department. It started small with a couple of police officers and a supervisor. Now we have a full-time Police Chief, a detective, and nine police officers. Still it's a small department by your experience."

"Charley, The General Store down the street, is it the old Lyle General Store?"

"No it was built in the fifties. The Lyle General Store burnt to the ground. Arson. People were scared. No one arrested for the murders and the more time that passed the stronger the belief that the killer must have been a Lyle. Many of the younger Lyles moved away to get out from under the suspicion. A few stayed. Most have died off. A few of Winfield Creek residents are distant descendants like the owner of The Grinder. Lyles are living in other counties and the harsh feeling towards the family is gone."

"No one today believes a member of the Lyle family had killed Thomas and his boys?"

"I didn't say that, Robert. There are plenty of theories about the killer, and some have the belief it was a family member, but no one has surmised which one."

"And what about this Lyle curse people say exists?" I asked.

"It's a crackpot notion that the Lyle family is cursed. It's a legend. Some say Timothy Lyle told the story to scare his enemies. The story is that in Scotland, during the middle ages, an Abbey of Monks turned to idol worship, and the devil appeared to them. He told the Monks if they swore allegiance to him he would give them the powers of sorcerers."

"How could the Monks powers of magic affect the Lyle family?" I interrupted.

"Patience, Robert. I'm getting there. A weary traveler stayed at the Abbey the night the devil appeared. The traveler, who believed the Abbey to be a holy place, had stumbled upon the wicked scene. He proceeded to chastise the Monks and threatened to expose their evil partnership. The Monks then decided to try out their newfound powers with a curse that tormented his mind. The traveler happened to be the Patriarch of the Lyle clan. Timothy's ancestor according to people who believe in this legend. The curse is on the family line, although, for unexplained reasons it doesn't affect every Lyle."

"It does sound silly and unbelievable. However, let's say a deranged family member could believe they are cursed. So what did the Patriarch do?" I said.

"It's been named the Cain curse. The Patriarch had been known as a righteous man turned to evil. He became a killer. One who had evaded detection for many years." I mulled over what Charley said.

"According to the story the curse is named after Adam's son, Cain, from the book of Genesis in the Bible, Robert."

"I get it, Charley. I've heard of the Bible."

Charley continued, "He killed his brother, Abel. For his crime, God cursed Cain to roam the earth with a mark on his forehead. The mark labeled him as the one who killed his brother, the righteous one. He and his descendants were outcasts. Moreover, he who killed Cain received the curse. It's said that the Monks' spell had put the same mark on the soul of the Patriarch and therefore on the ancestral line."

"How did Cain kill Abel?"

"He smashed his head with a stone," Charley said.

"So until now, Thomas Lyle and his sons were the only recorded murders in this town. Timothy's death had not been classified a murder," I said. "If this is a true story, and I'm not saying that it is, there would have been more killings and more dead bodies."

"That issue has been raised, and the so-called experts propose the bodies haven't been found yet. There are more than a few people who believe the Lyle family has the killer instinct," said Charley.

"Charley, I don't believe in magic spells or the devil for that matter, but I know evil when I see it. I don't like being the suspect, and I don't like the police detective either, he has it in for me."

"You're an outsider. People in Winfield Creek just don't trust outsiders."

"Do you trust me?"

"Until you give me a reason not to," Charley replied. "I'm pretty good at sizing people up. You don't smile much. You could smile a little more. People like a warm smile," Charley said.

"I smile inside," I said.

"Your eyes are like ice and folks don't see the smile inside," he said. "The police are under pressure to solve this case, Robert. The Mayor will apply pressure to the department until they make an arrest. She wants a conviction. Her son-in-law is the County District Attorney, and you happen to be the available suspect."

"You make a point, but they need evidence," I said.

"The fact you dated Marilyn may not be evidence, but it will keep them probing until they find some," Charley said. "Watch your back, Robert. Small town politics is brutal."

"Politics everywhere is brutal and sometimes lethal. I don't want to think this police force is desperate enough to fabricate evidence to satisfy the Mayor."

"I know Chief Bright, and I believe she would not do that, but I can't vouch for the other Police Officers," Charley said.

"You mean you can't vouch for the Detective," I said.

"I need to get back home," said Charley. "The hospice nurse will be leaving soon, and I can't leave Elizabeth by herself."

"How is she doing?"

"It's a matter of time, day to day. Cancer has ravished her body; if such a thing as a curse exists, then its cancer."

"I don't know how you handle it."

"Faith and unconditional love is the key. Have you ever been married?"

"Married to my career. The Army was my wife," I said.

"You're retired from the Army, and that might change things."

"It's not easy for a career bachelor to change," I said.

"When Elizabeth had been diagnosed with cancer, I had to change stride. Didn't like it. Wasn't easy, but where there is love, life comes into focus. The love between a man and a woman is unique. It's sacred, and it's not comparable to the love of a career." I looked away as Charley ended his sermon on love and marriage, "Don't underestimate our small but competent Police force. They are persistent."

"I am persistent too."

Charley stood to leave.

"I applied for my Private Investigator license." I have no idea why I blurted that out, but he grinned and shook his head.

"You said you were retired."

Chapter 3

Monday morning, I was determined to go on the offense. I parked a few blocks from the police station to use the walk time to think over my plan. I gazed through the library window, strolled past Harry's Barbershop, and practiced my pitch to Chief Bright.

Maybe she would jump at the chance and accept my help to find the killer. *Wishful thinking.* I'd have to convince her of the unique skill set I brought to the table: That I was not her prime suspect but her best asset.

Reynolds was a bigmouth, and I didn't see him as a problem. The ambitious Mayor Pickle was the wild card. Charley was right about political pressure. Her re-election posters covered every corner of the town. With the election on the horizon, the unsolved murder would work against her. Without an arrest, she would lose support from the Winfield Creek residents and push for an arrest—any arrest. Their fingers had already pointed to me.

If the Mayor believed, they had a case, no matter how flimsy the evidence, bagging me would cinch her reelection. I had to sway Chief Bright to my side. Would she buckle if Mayor Pickle demanded my arrest?

My life depended on Chief Bright being an honest cop.

Chapter 4

A middle-aged woman sat behind a long oak counter. I looked beyond her to a cluster of desks. Detective Reynolds was working the phone. To the left of his desk, I noticed an office door with large letters painted on its window **Chief Bright**.

Like most of the buildings in town, the police building was old. The floor was hardwood that had seen better days. The walls were covered with dingy plaster, wide baseboards, and decorative crown molding against a twelve-foot ceiling. The lights hung down from the ceiling on metal rods with large glass globes attached. On the opposite side of the room from Bright's office was the door that led to the cellblock. The place reminded me of Police Stations featured in old black and white films.

I gave the woman at the front desk my best smile. Charley was right; I didn't smile very much. My smiles looked like grins. "Excuse me. I would like to see Chief Bright."

Peering over her reading glasses, the woman said, "She is not available, Mr. Snow."

"Is this guy bothering you, Norma?" Detective Reynolds asked from behind his desk.

"No, Detective. We're fine," she said stridently. I got the feeling they didn't hang out together at the water cooler. Reynolds frowned and went back to his phone conversation.

"You know my name," I said.

"Mr. Snow, everyone knows who you are." Norma gestured to a church-like pew, "Have a seat. Would you like a cup of coffee?" I accepted her offer and sat down. Reynolds pulled his six-foot-plus frame up and paced like an angry bear. He studied a sheet of paper clutched in his large fist. I sipped the coffee. Norma wore a motherly smile.

"Thanks for the coffee. Do you think I'm a murderer too?"

"Everyone I know believes you are, Mr. Snow."

"I know one person who doesn't," I said.

"Excluding you," said Norma.

"Yes," I said. With a quizzical look, she returned to her desk.

"Charley Farber," I said.

"No surprise there, Mr. Snow, he's a Deacon. Isn't he supposed to refrain from judgment?"

"That's a good point, but according to Charley, that also goes for all of us."

"I'm just a police clerk, and I keep my opinions on who is guilty or not, to myself," Norma said.

"Norma, I will be out for a couple of hours," Reynolds said over his shoulder and exited through a back door. He grumbled under his breath.

"Is he always like that?" I asked Norma.

"Pretty much, Sam has a hard shell. I keep thinking that one of these days he'll let himself open up a bit."

I spent the next couple hours mulling over the architecture and watching people come in to pay parking tickets. Eventually, Chief Bright approached the counter.

"You want to see me?" she asked. She motioned to me, and I followed to her office. With her long-legged stride, she glided over the floor. A wave of her hand directed me to a seat in front of her desk. A sparsely decorated office fit her no-nonsense persona. Several awards hung on the wall behind her desk in black frames. Among them was an Honorable Discharge, a Winfield Creek High School Diploma, a B.A from the University of Tennessee and a Masters in Criminology from the University of Florida. The one window was adorned plain off-white curtains. Her desk was loaded with file folders piled six inches deep. There was a small vase of plastic flowers on a stand by the door. "Like the flowers," I said.

With a stern look and with an assertive tone she said, "What can I do for you? Make it quick, Mr. Snow. I'm busy."

"You had me followed, Chief?" I asked.

"Not yet. Why?"

"Saturday morning after Detective Reynolds had left the house I went for a run. And a man followed me."

"How do you know?" She asked.

"Training Chief." We gazed at one another, each sizing up the opposition. I decided to switch to small talk. "Were you born, and raised here?"

"Dad is career Army, Military Intel, and I was born in the Fort Knox hospital." Her demeanor softened. "Mom was born and raised in Winfield Creek. She moved us back here after she divorced Dad." She looked away. Her parents' divorce still bothered her.

"Army life is hard on families," I said.

"Why are you here, Mr. Snow?" Although she was easy on the eyes, she stood behind her desk like a spike. Her hands clenched, and her endless blue eyes locked on me.

"I want to apologize for my rude behavior on Saturday." She wasn't impressed. This woman was hard-hitting, in an attractive way.

"Don't patronize me, Mr. Snow. I know you. Your military record was exceptional, until the last year of your enlistment."

"You've read my file," I said.

"You made errors at Meade, Mr. Snow. Are you making more now?"

"There is more to my story than what's in the file," I said.

"Same with the murder." She flipped open a folder and slid it to me. Her slim fingers spread out several pictures. "Recognize her?" She chided.

A sigh parted my lips; I stared at the pictures without saying a word. The Tennessee Bureau of Investigation (TBI) forensic photographer captured a bloody scene. The woman I had dinner with last Friday night, lying in bed where someone had pummeled her head and face.

"Look familiar, Mr. Snow?"

"No, it doesn't," I said. "Did the crime scene provide any evidence?"

"Of course, you'd ask about that. You want to know what we know." She pulled an envelope from her desk and handed it to me. "These photographs arrived this morning," she said. I opened the envelope to see pictures of another murdered woman. A victim I knew too well.

"Mary Rinehart," I said. "My last case at CID and unsolved. I didn't find the killer or the murder weapon. No DNA, no evidence of any type recovered from the crime scene."

"And you had a relationship with this woman. According to this file, you delayed in reporting your personal involvement with the deceased to the Special Agents on the investigation team," said Chief Bright.

"I was the Special Agent in charge of the investigation. My relationship with her ended months before her murder, and everyone in the office had known about our affair," I said.

"How did she get in and why did she go to your house?"

"She still had a key, and I don't know why she had been at my house," I said.

"Disclosure is paramount! You had a personal connection with the case. That compromised your objectivity. Hiding information that's vital to the investigation is criminal. I don't know how you managed to avoid a court martial after striking your superior officer."

"Yeah, I slugged my superior who was also my friend. He suggested I had a vested interest in not solving the case."

"Mr. Snow, I have a murdered woman who has the same body build, hair color, and other shared characteristics with the victim at Meade."

"The MO was different," I said.

"You were involved with both women," Bright countered. "Two separate women, with similar features; both murdered, and they dated the same man. You expect me to assume it was a coincidence?" Bright's tone rose to a little less than a scream.

I didn't reply. This meeting was not going according to plan.

I softened my tone and said, "Okay, you have the connections to get my file. My ex-friend and superior is Colonel Marston. I lost control and slugged him. Colonel Marston cut me a deal: retire or court martial."

She smiled. "A couple of months after you moved in, we have a murder and you were involved with the victim. Just like the case at Fort Meade."

I sat back in my chair and exhaled. "Yes, Mary and I had a romance. Does Reynolds know about that case?" I asked.

"What do you think?" She said.

"He has it in for me, you know."

"For now, I'm keeping this to myself. Don't ask why because I won't tell you."

I looked at the pictures of Marilyn Todd again. She seemed peaceful, in a macabre kind of way.

Bright closed the folder. "Forensics did not find a weapon or foreign prints. No visible sign of forced entry, the blood splatter is consistent with a blunt instrument. The two crime scenes are similar but different." I was glad she was sharing information with me.

"In both cases the killer scrubbed the crime scene. Mary Rinehart took a bullet to the head, and Marilyn Todd was bludgeoned to death. The lethal methods were different in each case, but you know as well as I do, killers every now and then change their MO. I want to know everything you remember about the Meade case," Bright said.

"I can do better than that, Chief. I have copies of notes and interviews packed in a box at my house. Come over tonight and we can go through them together. I'll cook dinner." She kept her eyes on the folder. She pretended not to hear the invitation.

"Sounds like you and I are collaborating," I said to break the silence. "I'd like nothing better than to help you find the killer. But I need Reynolds off my back."

"From where he stands, you're a dirty cop. We had one here a few years back. He and Sam were high school friends. They came on the force together, but his friend turned to pushing Meth. We don't have a murder rate in Winfield Creek, but we have Meth labs and pot farms. As you know Mr. Snow, some killers are known to insert themselves into the investigation of their crimes." Then she looked me in the eye for several long, uncomfortable, seconds. "But we might be able to help each other." I waited.

"Report everything you discover to me." I nodded in agreement. Then she added, "This way, I can keep my eye on you." She handed me the file.

I stood, and started towards her office door when she called out, "You don't have the right name."

"What do you mean?"

"You applied to the state for your Private Investigator license."

"Yes, I did."

"Snow is not a tough guy name," she said.

"Deception," I said. "People underestimate me all the time. Most Private Investigators aren't tough guys. That's from books and television."

"I don't leave 'til after six. Can't make it tonight."

"Don't worry. I'll call you." I closed the door behind me. I wasn't sure if she viewed me as a serial killer or a potential date.

Chapter 5

With a hot cup of black tea, a highlighter, my favorite chair, and soft jazz on the Bose, I sat back to study the preliminary report on Marilyn's murder. I read Officer O'Connor's observations starting when he arrived at the house and his impressions of the crime scene during his walk-through.

The 9-1-1 dispatcher logged the call, from Mason Dew, at zero six hundred July third two-thousand and thirteen. O'Connor arrived on scene at zero six ten. You can drive from one end of town to the other in ten minutes, and that is in traffic. "In Winfield Creek, heavy traffic is more than six cars going one direction," I chuckled.

Bumper to bumper traffic happened to be a large deterrent in my decision not to return to Northern California, but not the main reason. I hadn't been back since mom and dad's funerals. An addict killed them during a home invasion robbery. He was after drug money the homicide detective had said. Back from Nam two months when it happened. I was numb. Everything they owned, I had shoved in a storage locker. My boyhood home placed with a property manager, I headed back to Carson, my real home.

That was a long time ago. Focus on the here and now. The county Medical Examiner estimated the time Marilyn had died was after midnight and before zero five hundred.

Was the killer in the house waiting when she thanked me for an enjoyable evening? On the other hand, he could have hidden close by waiting for me to leave.

She had excused herself saying she planned to go straight to bed. If she had invited me inside, maybe Marilyn would still be alive, or maybe we'd both be dead.

She was a remarkable woman. Her personality electrified my senses. Nothing else mattered when we were together. I shook her image from my head and concentrated on the report.

Detective Reynolds was on the scene right after O'Connor, and Chief Bright arrived twenty minutes later. Another patrol officer arrived on scene at O'Connor's request for backup. I made a note. Why did he need backup? I reached for the tea, but it had already turned cold. I sat the cup down and pondered over the report.

Two hours later, my eyes started to blur. From my pocket I fished a bottle of eye drops, lubed my eyes, and then I forced myself to continue. I highlighted and annotated several more sections of information to follow up on, and then I bolted upright, angry. A witness statement to the police described a woman who had run from the Todd house on the morning of the murder.

"Bright didn't tell me they had a witness. Detective Reynolds came to my house, busted my chops, accusing me; even though, they had this Mason Dew guy who saw a woman leave the scene of the crime," I shouted at the furniture.

After warming up the cold cup of tea, I let the soothing aroma fill my nostrils for twenty minutes to clear the mad spell from my system. Chief Bright knew when she handed over the report I would see the witness statement. She could have warned me. She knew I would be mad. How could I trust Bright when she was not forthcoming? She kept the file on the Meade case from her detective. There are reasons not to share information, and it revolves around trust. I knew why she didn't trust me, but where was her faith in Reynolds? My cell phone startled me,

"Hello."

"Are you reading the prelim?" Laura Bright asked.

"Yes, you call all of your suspects late at night?"

"Ten is not late."

"Time is twenty-two thirty, and it's late when you get up at zero four hundred," I said. "I have concerns with the report."

"What part?" She said.

"You damn well know what part."

"The witness saw a female suspect running from the scene of the crime," Bright said. I worked hard to keep my mouth shut. "At the time, that was information you did not need to know," she added.

"You had a prime suspect when Reynolds came to my house and treated me like the killer. I don't like it," I said, struggling to control the tone of my voice.

"You don't have to like it, Snow. You were with the victim the evening before the murder. I wanted your honest reaction to Todd's death. I have a knack for reading people. I won't apologize for stepping on your ego to get the information I need."

"I can take it, but I still don't like it," I said. Her tone was firm and assertive. This woman did not take crap. I was starting to like her.

Bright continued to talk. "We haven't located the woman Dew

described. Until we do, anyone connected to Marilyn Todd is a person of interest."

"Any other surprises I should know about?" I said.

"Keep reading and we'll talk tomorrow. You're a civilian now. Dump the military time." She hung up.

Dew described the suspect to be about five foot eight. She wore a dark sweat top, shorts, and running shoes. She had long red hair pulled back with a white sweatband. Approximate age thirty to forty. The report stated Dew saw her skip down the front steps in a hurry. She had left the front door open, and Dew shouted at her. She bolted east towards downtown. O'Connor did not note if the suspect carried anything.

On the cell, I opened www.sunsetsunrise.com: the sun rose at zero six twenty-three. The 911 operator received the call at zero six hundred; therefore, it was still relatively dark when Dew saw the suspect. Dew gave the police a detailed description of the woman. He had a keen eye in the dark. I continued to read and highlighted the elements that stuck out. The back door, off the kitchen, locked. An interior door off the living room, locked. The report emphasized the cleanliness of the kitchen, dining room, and living room. Neat and clean, that was my impression also. When I picked Marilyn up for our dinner date, she had invited me in while she changed purses.

The report says there had been no sign of forced entry. Marilyn had opened the door for someone she knew. Unaware that she had invited the killer into her home, I thought.

Officer O'Connor described the murder scene in the upstairs bedroom as horrific. Her bloodied body laid in the bed, under the top sheet with her arms folded across her stomach. Blood splattered on the headboard and the wall behind the bed. Her pillow and the bed covers were soaked with blood, no visible signs of a struggle. O'Connor's observation was that Marilyn had been asleep when the killer struck the fatal blows.

My heart ached with the description. This type of brutality suggested rage. Her body was lying in a solemn repose. Did the killer position her to look like she was asleep?

The bedroom was sparsely furnished. A nightstand by the bed and a dresser against the opposite wall. The report did not mention pictures or decorative items. I guessed there weren't any, as in the rooms downstairs. Nothing was out of place, and her money and credit cards were in her purse. That ruled out robbery as a viable motive. Off the bedroom was a full bath with the usual toiletries. A walk-in closet contained only four sets of clothing. Marilyn lived a minimalist life. O'Connor made a point to emphasize that nothing seemed out of place.

No blood stains on the carpet. The carpet looked vacuumed. A smart killer would have cleaned the vacuum hose, emptied the chamber, and removed the filters. Then she would have had to get rid of them. Except the suspect that the witness described running away did not carry anything with her. "I need to talk to this witness," I said aloud.

The last paragraph revealed something else. When O'Connor walked out of the bedroom, he saw Mason Dew in the foyer. Standard procedure would be for Dew to wait outside for the Detective. Why did Dew go inside? Curiosity? Chief Bright had said that some criminals revisit the scene of the crime and even try to insert themselves in the investigation.

A separate document in the file was a property deed. Marilyn Todd purchased the house in 2011. I wasn't sure if this document had any significance, but it was interesting that Marilyn had bought the house two years before she moved. She had hidden that from me.

She said she bought a house in Winfield Creek about the same time I did. She gave me the impression that she had not been to Winfield Creek before that time. She said, 'East Tennessee seemed like a good place.'

Another note was attached to the preliminary report about the autopsy. Criminal background checks on Dew and Todd were pending. With a few finger taps on the iPad, I prioritized my notes and set reminders. The number one item on my task list was to have a talk with Mr. Mason Dew. Then I had to get inside Marilyn's house. Maybe the lab techs overlooked something. After that, I would meet with Chief Bright to compare notes and share assumptions.

As I shut the file, I couldn't help but think Robert Snow is back.

Chapter 6

After my Tuesday morning run, I headed out in search of Mason Dew. The Bean Pot Motel was a dive. Trash was scattered everywhere. The building was in a state of disrepair, and the sign had been overgrown with honeysuckle. There were two vehicles in the parking lot. The place was a haven for winos, druggies, and one-night whores. I parked in the middle of the lot facing the rooms.

A bell dinged overhead when I pushed open the office door. A dense layer of tobacco and booze burned my nose. A fat elderly woman sat behind the counter. A low cut patch of rags for clothes revealed more of her large frame than I wanted to see. She smelled as though she hasn't bathed in months. She raised her eyes from a Playgirl magazine.

"Hey," she drawled, through one side of her mouth. A plume of acrid smoke rose from the corncob pipe clenched between her two discolored teeth. She laid the Playgirl mag on the counter and said, "We're full up."

"Parking lot is near empty," I said. "And I don't need a room. Here to see Mr. Mason Dew."

"You the law?" she said. "He rob somebody or sellin' drugs?"

"I consult with the police, and I need to talk to him. I know he checked in here," I said, impatiently. She grumbled, and another plume of smoke rose from her pipe.

"He's in Room 5, and don't snoop around anywhere else," she said, picking up her magazine. I opened the door to leave the office when she called out, "You hung like this feller?" She held up the centerfold, and I glared at the photo. Her laugh sounded like a cross between a saxophone and a hyena. She waddled from behind the counter. I hurried from the office and fast walked to room 5. I looked back. The fat woman went back inside. Relieved, I knocked on Dew's door. A skinny man of average height opened the door the length of the security chain. He stared blankly through dilated pupils.

"Special Agent Robert Snow, CID," I identified myself and flashed my military identification card; "I would like to ask you a few questions, Mr. Dew." I stowed my ID before Dew could ask to have a closer look and discover I was retired.

"About what?" he stuttered.

"The woman you saw running from the murder scene, Saturday morning."

"Don't know her," He said and pushed the door back in my face. I stuck my foot between the door and post. I grinned at Mason Dew.

"How did you know my name? Who did you say you are?" He asked.

"You heard me the first time, and I showed you my identification. I have a few questions about the murder; I won't take much of your day." A shadow moved behind Dew, and I heard a door open and shut.

"Told the real police everything I know." His tone was agitated.

"May I come in?" With my foot wedged between the door and the jamb, Dew had little choice. He frowned then stepped back, unhooked the chain.

The floor was littered with beer cans. The air smelled like vomit. The bed covers were balled up in a pile. A laptop sat on the bureau. A used condom was on the floor by the bed. No drugs were in plain view, but there were no doubts in my mind Dew was on the downside of a high. Dew walked over and leaned his back against the bathroom door. His arms folded against his chest. I figured the bathroom was where his drug-buddy whore was hiding.

"How did you happen to be at the scene of the crime?" I was tempted to pull out my handkerchief to filter the stench that made my voice hoarse.

"I was hiking the Appalachian Trail and stopped at Winfield Creek to resupply," Dew said with a ring of nervousness in his voice. "I was heading back to the trail."

"Why this motel, when there are better places closer to town?" I said.

"This motel isn't that far from town. The daily rate is cheap." I already knew the real answer before I asked the next question.

"Wasn't it the supply of prostitutes and drugs and not the cheap rate that drew you to the Bean Pot?" The question rattled Dew. His eyes narrowed, and he rubbed his arms. "Relax, I'm not here to bust you, but I need answers."

"The walk out to here is trivial compared to the miles on the trail. I'm not a regular user. Just some liquor and pot once in a while for a high time," Dew added.

"Nevertheless," I said, "why did you take a route down Little Bear when the direct route to the trail goes straight through the center of town? It seemed, to me, that when one planned a trek that's about two thousand miles long to add additional distance is inefficient."

"My hike started in Resaca Georgia and will end in Bennington, Vermont. That's 976 miles. I was on that side of town because it's a side street with less traffic. Are you about done? I need to get back to it," he said.

"Looks like you had a party in here last night. By yourself, Mr. Dew?"

"I had a few beers and some weed," he said.

"Alone?" I said again. Dew was a real slob. His hair was matted. Food was stuck in his mangy beard, and he must have just thrown clothes on when I knocked. "Just one more question, if I may. Why did you come back here?" He shuffled his feet and swayed backwards.

"The police told me to stay in town for a while. In case they need me to identify the woman."

"Of course," I said. "They haven't found her yet. Mind if I use your bathroom before I leave?"

"Yes, I do mind," he said. "Use the one at the office. Now if you're finished, please go." He hurried past me and opened the door.

"No problem. By the way, the police are right. You need you to stay around until we sort this out."

"I am on a tight schedule, Mr. Snow. I need to be in Vermont before winter, or I will be stuck on the mountain in bad weather. My wife will be waiting for me in Bennington."

"Oh, you're married then?" I looked to the bathroom door. "How long have you been a Thru-Walker, Mr. Dew?

"What? Oh yes, It had been on my bucket list for years. I decided it's now or never," he said.

"Call your wife, and tell her you're delayed." Dew stiffened and shot me a disgusted glance.

I turned in the doorway. "One last question, Mr. Dew. Your description of the suspect was good. Did you happen to remember any other details about her?" He rolled his eyes up,

"Just that she had tattoos, a lot of them on her hands and arms, neck and her legs."

"Did she carry a pack or anything else?"

"No," he said. "Nothing."

"Thank you, Mr. Dew. By the way, I didn't see any equipment."

Dew stammered, "I stored my gear in a locker at the general store."

I gave him a puzzled look, and then walked outside. I headed towards the Explorer. Dew watched from a window until I started the engine. Mr. Mason Dew had more explaining to do. I had known plenty of backpackers over the years, and he was no backpacker. Next stop was the General Store to confirm Dew had rented a locker and then to the station.

Chapter 7

I stood across the street from Marilyn's house. At zero five hundred, it was still dark. The boxwoods that lined the front of her house were hard to see. I was near the spot where Mason Dew stood when he saw the woman run from the house. There was little chance Dew could have seen the woman's tattoos or determined her hair color. I suspected Dew had lied to the police.

The driveway was to the right of Marilyn's house. The house to the left was where Jessie lived. As he had said, the small window between the first and second floor had a line of sight to the front porch. I scanned the houses behind me, and both ways on the street, to make sure no one else was around. I pulled the stocking mask down over my face, stepped away from the oak, and crossed the street towards the driveway. The neighborhood was quiet.

In a dozen long strides, I reached the driveway. The black nylon outfit allowed me to blend into the blackness between the houses. The planned entry point was the rear door that led into the kitchen. Breaking into Marilyn's house was a huge risk. One I had to take. I could have no hiccups, and had to be out before sunrise. If a neighbor called the police, it would be *game over*. Reynolds would collect his prize.

Getting inside was easy. Authentic Victorian homes aren't equipped with sophisticated door locks. After checking for a security alarm, my tools made quick work of the door. I ducked under the yellow police tape and crept into the kitchen.

I moved through the kitchen, and without warning, my thoughts dredged up Reynolds. The image produced a burst of anger. My heart raced. "Why did I think of him?" I mumbled. "I'm letting him get inside my head."

I stopped and redirected my feelings. After a few moments of slow breathing, my anxiety dissipated. Chief Bright came to mind. She would be pissed if she found out what I was doing.

Breathe—in and out—she will never know.

I had no idea what I was looking for. TBI had processed the crime scene, and they have a good rep, but even seasoned crime scene technicians miss the proverbial needle in the haystack, sometimes.

With a penlight, I ducked under a small kitchen window along a row of cabinets to the archway between the kitchen and the dining room. There were no windows in the dining room, and I could stand up and give my knees relief. They cracked like eggshells. The pen light reflected off a glass globe that hung over a dining room set that included an empty china cabinet and a serving table on the side. There were no pictures or decorative items hung on the walls. That seemed unusual. Women like to make things warm and cute. This room felt cold and unattractive. It didn't fit Marilyn's personality.

I low crawled into the front room staying below the double hung windows. I had been in here before. I remembered Marilyn's full lips, that infectious smile, her blue jeans, and her blouse. She had made casual look classy. I forced her image from my head and pocketed the pen light. The first glimpse of sunrise illuminated the sheer drapes that covered the front windows, and the threat of being exposed grew stronger. I had more area to cover, but I needed to leave soon or stay until sundown. That wasn't an option.

At the top of the stairs, the door to Marilyn's bedroom was open. My anxiety built again as the bedroom door triggered a mental image of Marilyn's bloodied body. I bit down on my knuckle until my brain redirected to the pain and removed the image from my thoughts. Being in this house was harder than I had anticipated. I pulled myself together and then moved toward the stairs.

A slight movement froze me in place. I turned my head and noticed the gentle sway of the window curtain behind the love seat. A fist sized hole cut in the windowpane above the locks. The window was open a few inches off the sill. I was not alone in the house.

How did I miss that open window when I approached? I thought and leaned against an overstuffed chair.

My position gave me an unobstructed line of sight to the stairs. Nevertheless, I couldn't stay still. Daylight was coming fast. I had to go on the offense, find the intruder, and neutralize him or her. I patted the inside holster on my left hip. My hands trembled. *What is going on with me?*

Reassured the 45 was still in place, I started to make my move. Then I heard a noise, like metal scraping against metal. It came from the room adjacent to the staircase. My veins swelled with adrenaline. I was ready for action. I reached for the 45 and then stopped. *Gunfire would alert the neighbors and bring the police down on us. It would be easier to explain my intrusion if I had a live suspect in custody.*

I low-crawled toward the room and stopped when the door opened. I moved backward. My position was not exposed. A person dressed in black clothing exited the room. The muscular frame indicated male, and he carried something in his right hand. I watched as he moved from the room, unconcerned with the budding sunlight streaming through the windows, and then he turned towards me. I was between him and the open window. He didn't see me. I knew I couldn't allow him to leave the house. His body type appeared to be close to mine. If he was armed, the timing had to be perfect. I couldn't give him room to make a run for it or to pull a gun and shoot my ass. I had the element of surprise.

The black-clad intruder crossed my path and instinct took over. Like a cat, I sprang leading with my left shoulder and plowed him with my full weight. The attack threw him off balance. I caught him by surprise. We rolled, grunting like hogs, I grappled to employ an armbar hold, and his wide eyes behind the black ski mask made me feel good, confident.

Like lighting, the man recovered, blocked my ability to control his arms, and swung his leg over my back. He hooked my waist with his heel and rolled me over before I could counter. Lying face up on top of him with his legs locked around my stomach. My arms were free. Then, I felt the impact of an object on my head. My vision blurred. Strength fled from me like air escaping a balloon.

Chapter 8

A foot nudged my side. My vision was blurred, the pain was splitting my head, and my arms locked behind my back were numb. I noticed the faint outline of a uniformed police officer standing over me.

"Good. He's waking up." A large man walked over, stood, and looked down, laughing.

"This is like winning the lottery. Agent Bob all dressed in black and hog tied." Reynolds stooped down. "Guess you know burglary and tampering with a crime scene is a serious offense. All I can say is I like what I see," he bellowed.

"You don't have me on burglary, Sherlock," I managed to say.

"How did you get your head busted open? Stumble on the window sill?" Reynolds said. "A citizen called it in when they saw the open window. The guilty man returns to the scene of the crime. Just like in the movies. Not real smart, Agent Bob."

"Are you going to read me my rights, Detective?"

He turned to the uniformed officer. "Read him, get him out of here, and book him for breaking and entering. Call Doc Hudson to stitch up his head wound." Reynolds turned his head back to look at me, and for a second, I thought he would tap dance.

Chapter 9

"I didn't know what hit me," I said. "Laura, I went to the house and entered through the back door."

"First, don't address me by my first name and second, why did you break into the Todd house in the first place?"

"I needed to see it for myself. To be sure the lab techs didn't miss anything."

"I told you to keep me informed. On the phone, I had said we would discuss the prelim in the office. You did not show. If you needed to see inside the house, why didn't you come and ask me?"

"Would you have agreed?"

"No," she said. Anger filled her eyes.

"I know this makes you look bad, having given me the benefit of the doubt, but the person who busted my head removed something from that house that may be crucial evidence. We need to find who took it and what it is. I'm not your killer," I said, "Who called it in?"

"Thelma Burke. She lives on the block. Heaven help me, Snow. You were caught at the crime scene dressed up like a Ninja."

"Somebody knocked me unconscious."

"Sam's theory is you banged your head climbing in through the window. He is hard at work to prove you returned to the scene of the crime to retrieve the murder weapon."

"That's ridiculous. I have six stitches in my head, and my blood is not on the window. Any numskull can figure out I didn't split my head open on the window." Impatience made my tone stronger than I intended. "Reynolds could be right about the killer returning to retrieve the murder weapon. The object the intruder carried appeared to be square and metal."

"Let's suppose I believed you. How did the intruder get the drop on you?"

"He didn't. I initiated the attack," I said.

"Your close-quarters skills are rusty," she said and turned on her tablet. After a couple of finger swipes, she leaned closer. "This is the crime scene map and inventory. No wall hangings of any type anywhere. The rooms are furnished with typical items and the standard utensils in the kitchen. The basement contained a furnace, water heater, washer, and dryer. This compare with what you found in the house?"

"Yeah, I didn't go into the basement or get to the bedrooms. The door, described in the preliminary report as adjacent to the living room and locked, is where the intruder came from. My entry point was the back door to the kitchen. In the living room, I saw the window with the hole in the pane above the locks. The window was raised about two inches. That's when I knew someone else had been or was in the house. I low-crawled through the living room when I heard the sound, a few minutes later the door opened, and the intruder came out." Bright listened, and she did not say a word. "You have to get me out of here, Chief. I can't help you from this cell."

"Your stunt put you in this cell. Sam will load up the B&E with more charges. He is hard around the edges, and he does not like you. He believes you're the killer, a dirty cop."

"He may make the breaking and entering stick. Murder charges, no way. Without evidence, he's spinning his wheels," I said. "I know you will do the right thing. You won't allow political pressure to cloud your reasoning." Without another word, she left the cellblock.

Chapter 10

"Morning Sam," Chief Bright said. She entered the bullpen with a confident gait. Her smile faded when she saw me sitting outside her office. "Twenty folks showed up in Mayor Pickle's office this morning and demanded justice. The Mayor is in a pickle, Sam; pun intended," she said with a gentle laugh. "The concerned residents were led by Thelma Burke demanding to know why the killer is still walking around town and not charged with murder." She paused and stared right at me. Sam remained quiet and shot me a glance.

"Chief—"

"Why are you here, Mr. Snow?" she interrupted. I followed her into her office. "Close the door." She said it loud enough for Reynolds to hear. She sat her coffee cup on the desk. With her small voice, she said, "Charley paid your bail?"

"I already reimbursed him," I said.

"Sam is peeved. I told him I busted your chops in the cell. The charges he can lay on you are the B&E, and that is thin. Nothing listed on the inventory is missing from the house. Sam combed over it three times. You saw how sparse that place was."

"Not much there to steal," I said. "That's odd, a woman with no pictures or decorations. Four sets of clothes in the closet and an empty china cabinet?"

"It's strange," Laura said, looking around her office.

"An office is one thing, but her home?"

"You saw the copy of the property deed. She bought the house two years before moving here, and the house was never vacant. An old widower lived there, John Sampson. He sold the house to Todd but still lived there until he died," Laura said.

"Marilyn moved in after he died?" I asked.

"A month after he was buried, to be exact. Sampson had kept to himself. He was friendly when you saw him and spoke if he had to. A real estate and property management company in Knoxville handled the sale, Lyn Realty."

"Checked them out yet?"

"Sam visited them. They were cooperative and provided copies of the sale agreement," she said.

"When did his wife die?" I said.

"2010. I don't understand why that's important."

"Just curious. O'Connor noted in the prelim that the bedroom carpet looked as though it had been vacuumed."

"Yeah, the killer did a good job scrubbing the crime scene. The carpet is cleaner than the one downstairs."

"Did the vacuum cleaner get tagged and the bag checked?"

"The vacuum is the bagless type, and the waste baskets were empty. Hoses washed out, and the sink drains cleaned with Drano. The killer knew how to clean and stage a crime scene. She was careful."

"Still thinking about the woman Mason Dew described? The problem is she didn't tote anything away from the scene. She emptied the vacuum. Where is the garbage bag?" I said.

"That is a problem. Oh, before I forget to tell you, Sam found a piece of black nylon fabric snagged on a small nail, on the windowsill. He danced with joy until he couldn't find a tear in your outfit."

"It's like I said—"

"Sam hates you," she finished my sentence.

"He's not the first one. Don't suppose blood showed up anywhere other than the bedroom?"

"No blood stains on the carpet by the bed or the stairs," Bright said. "I went to the house and checked out the den. By the tracks in the carpet, I knew someone had moved the Personal Computer tower. The intruder had removed the screws on the back cover. I set the cover aside and discovered a loose hard drive cable. My thought was the computer had a second hard disk. A hard drive is metal and would make a nice gash on your head."

"How did that get missed in the crime scene investigation?" I said.

"The PC hadn't been moved, and the back cover was closed."

"The crime scene techs would have booted the computer. They should have seen the second hard drive icon," I said.

"With the cable unplugged, there's no power to the hard drive, and it couldn't boot. Therefore no drive icon," she said. "The hard drive must have contained some serious information for someone to break into a crime scene to steal it."

"Do you think the intruder knew Marilyn had the information on that drive and he killed her for it," I asked.

"Then why not take the hard drive after he killed Marilyn? It doesn't make sense to me he would leave without it."

"The woman who ran from the house spooked him," I offered.

"Or she may be working with the man who broke in and took the hard drive."

"You think the woman killed Marilyn? Then something happened to prevent her from retrieving the disk drive. Therefore, her accomplice had to burglarize the house to get it."

"Just thinking out loud," Bright said.

"What had Marilyn been involved in?" I wonder.

"She may not have been the sweet innocent woman she led you to believe, Robert."

"What else is going on here? It may be more than just a murder investigation now. By the way, I had a talk with Mason Dew," I said.

"You're just now telling me this?" she snarled.

"I didn't have an opportunity. Too busy getting arrested," I grinned. "Mason said the woman had tattoos on her arms and legs. He withheld that from your Officer. Maybe he purposely misled the police."

"Oh, don't worry. We knew about the tattoos." I cocked my head. "It's a small town, Robert. The woman he described still hasn't come up on our APB," she said.

"She may not exist," I responded.

"What else did he say?"

"Not much, but I know he is not a hiker," I said. Bright stood and walked to her office door. She instructed Norma to call Sam and have him bring Mason Dew in for a follow-up report.

"If his official statement is full of holes, we'll find them. How does the head feel, Robert?"

"It's sore, but I'll live. I suspected he had a woman in the room. She ducked into the bathroom to avoid me seeing her."

"What do you make of that?"

"He's married, and she was the one night stand. However, if he turned out to be the killer, then she could have been his accomplice. They may have staged her to run from the scene."

"Then he pretended to be a witness?"

"Like you said before Chief, some real sick serial killers get a thrill from inserting themselves into the investigation," I said.

"Serial killer is not a word I want to be spread around town. Residents are scared." She examined my head. "Doc did a good job stitching up your wound. Still looks like a grapefruit."

"Golf ball size and I've had worse."

"You think Dew gave you the head knocker?"

"No way, he's a wimp. The guy that took me down is a pro."

"Is that your ego talking?" She smiled.

"In my day I could hold my own with anyone. A few years of age slowed me down some. I just need to use brains more than muscle," I said.

"Uh-huh, and it's more than a few years."

"These residents have a right to be scared," I said. "It was a horrific murder, committed either from spontaneous rage or by a psychopath. We don't have anything to go on."

"We have two suspects: you and the woman Dew saw," she said.

"Good luck with that," I said.

"The Press editorials, the Knox Sentinel, and our local Bugle criticized this department and questioned my professional skills. The mayor reads those articles. She is not a patient woman." Bright tossed the paper across the desk at me, "I said to keep me informed."

"Are we going through that again? You already gave me hell for it."

"I can give you hell anytime I choose," she said. "I'm still pissed. What else have you not told me?"

"I can cook. Maybe you need to keep me closer, keep a good eye on me," I grinned.

"Damn you! Do not get fresh with me." Her face glowed crimson. I half expected her to pull her weapon and shoot me. Instead, she threw her hands in the air, sighed, and then said, "Tell me more about why you think our witness is a liar."

"If he was backpacking the Appalachian Trail, as he claimed, he would have the gear for it. I asked him about that, and he said he had stored his gear in a locker. I went to the General Store to check it out. Those lockers are large enough to hold a trail-ready pack, but Mason Dew did not rent one."

"The prelim didn't mention he had a backpack," she said.

"I didn't see a pack in his motel room. His reason for being on Little Bear Lane does not sit right with me either. If he had headed back to the mountain, efficiency dictates he should take the most direct route through town. Dew selected a street that took him a mile out of his way. Besides, he's too puny to carry a sixty-pound pack on the trail. Mason Dew lied."

"If not a witness, then is he the killer?"

"Can't rule out the possibility," I said." But I doubt he had the gumption to have killed Marilyn. My bet is he knew the killer. Another thing, I was thinking about the clean carpet. The killer could have used plastic to cover the floor around the bed?"

"Then why vacuum?" Bright said, "Any hair and skin particles from the victim and the assailant would have been on the plastic."

"Our killer was smart. We don't know how long he messed with the body." Laura was horrified, but she knew. There are serial killers who violate corpses. "It appeared to me her body was posed."

"Nothing can be ruled out until we have the full autopsy report to verify theories. We won't rule out Dew was the killer either. If he did kill Marilyn and then acted as a witness, he had stone-cold nerves," Laura said.

"The man I spoke with was timid," I said. "Mason Dew was anything but stone-cold."

"Maybe he's a good actor," Laura said.

"Possible. You need to lean on him hard when Sam brings him in," I said. "Also, you need to make sure the M.E. does a drug screen on Marilyn's body. If he spent the time covering the floor, there's no way he could have done that without waking her, and that means she wasn't asleep. When I stood across the street from Marilyn's house, the same time of morning Dew did, I could not see well enough to distinguish a woman's hair color. What bothers me more about Dew's description is that the woman had been dressed for a jog, not to commit a premeditated and a very bloody murder."

"Think so Robert? We thought the killer acted from spontaneous anger?"

"Rage could describe it, but I believe it was premeditated. I believe the woman is real, and she is someone Dew knows."

"An accomplice," Chief Bright replied.

"You're getting to like me, Laura."

"Why do you say that?"

"You asked about my wound, how I feel, and you use my first name when talking to me."

"You kind of grow on a person, like a wounded puppy. In the office, call me Chief. I don't want anyone getting the wrong impression."

"Humph," I grunted. "We also need to know more about Marilyn Todd."

"Hope you didn't get too fond of her, Robert," Chief Bright said.

"I'm good." I stood and walked towards the door. Reynolds passed as I exited.

"Detective." I tried to smile, but didn't have it in me to be cordial. He pushed past me without acknowledging my presence. I stopped and looked back while he spoke to Chief Bright. I could tell by her body language that Reynolds did not have good news.

Chapter 11

I pushed the double glass doors open to exit the station and almost collided with Charley Farber. He was in a hurry.

"Robert."

"What's up Charley?"

"Glad I ran into you, Robert. I'm worried about my son, David." Charley was a calm soul, but he seemed agitated.

"Okay. If you need to talk I have the time," I said.

"He has this girlfriend. It's suspicious," he said.

"Having a girlfriend is suspicious? Is that just an overprotective father talking?"

"I mean, she looked suspicious?"

"Let's walk over to the Grinder and talk over a cup of coffee," I said.

"No, it's too crowded, curious ears, Robert. Hard to have privacy in this town, talking in a public place, you might as well broadcast our conversation on the radio. Let's go over to the church."

"Not sure about that Charley."

"I have an office," he said. I walked with him to the Church. The size of his office resembled a prison cell. It had modest furnishings and to my surprise just two religious items: a crucifix hung on the wall behind his desk and a portrait of the Pope hung above the file cabinet. "Have a seat, Robert." He left for a minute and returned with two cups of coffee. "Not like the Grinder's coffee." I took the cup and Charley shut the office door. He sat down in the high back leather chair. His face was a mask of concern. "David and I don't see eye to eye on many things. We used to before Elizabeth got sick. I've tried to reach out to repair the hard feelings between us, but he didn't acknowledge me. I can't talk to him. So I watched from a distance."

"You followed him?"

"Yes, to make sure he's alright. I know how that sounds. It's despicable, but I needed to see him. This morning I drove over to Knoxville. It had been a couple of weeks since my last trip. I saw her with David. She is not the type of woman my son should be spending time with, Robert."

"Not being a father I don't know what you're feeling, except I can imagine it's hard." The right words to say were beyond my expertise. I had a good relationship with my father, but like most father and son relationships it had been rocky at times. "Don't understand how I can help you with this one, Charley."

"Something about her does not sit right. She's much older. What could she want with a kid?"

"I can think of a few possibilities." The reaction on Charley's face changed my failed attempt to interject humor to a serious tone. "But I wouldn't know for sure."

"Not just older, but she is covered with tattoos and piercings. She looked evil," Charley said.

The mention of tattoos got my attention, "How old is David?"

"Twenty-one,"

"Charley, he's a man and he can do what he wants. Why were you going to the police?" I said.

"I heard about the description of the woman running from the Todd house. She had tattoos."

"How did you hear that? I just told the Chief a few minutes ago."

"It's small town, Robert.

"So I've been told, several times," I said. "Suppose I can check her out, and if this woman fits the description of the person we're looking for, then I will report her to Chief Bright. Nevertheless, her description is on the wire, and it's hard to believe she'd be in Knoxville, and not spotted by the police. This woman has what color hair?"

"I don't know. She shaved her head. She looked rough," Charley said.

"Did David have a tendency towards older women?" I said.

"I don't know. This is the first woman I had seen him with since he graduated from high school. He's not a bad looking guy. He can do better."

"You can't make a man be who he doesn't want to be," I said.

"David hasn't been himself since Elizabeth got sick. Heck, I'm not my old self either."

"Understandable," I said.

"She had fought cancer for ten years. In remission more than once, and it came back like a thief in the night. We had been blessed with more time together then some, but I want more. Faith gets us through, but David had thrown his faith away. David stopped going to Mass, said he no longer believed in God. Life is evil, he said. That woman looked like a Jezebel."

"I don't know Charley. You are the religious guy. I never saw the need to believe in anything I can't see or touch."

"You're intelligent, Robert. You can—"

"I don't know anything about religion, Charley. Mom and Dad didn't raise me that way. I do know evil when I see it. People commit evil deeds, and I have spent most of my life bringing them to justice. The problem is there are always more. Like zombies, they keep on coming. As your friend, I will check her out. David has a car?"

"Old Pontiac Firebird, black. I don't know the license plate number. He lives in a rundown apartment house on Fifth Ave. Not the best side of town."

"I'll check it out. Give me a couple of days," I said. Charley appeared relieved, "If the woman is our suspect, I'll notify Chief Bright.

Chapter 12

Friday morning traffic was manic. "What the heck's going on?" I said.

"This murder has gone viral," Laura said.

"Why?"

"It's all over Facebook, Twitter, Google+, You-Tube. Every amateur crime-buster is in town and they post their theories on social media."

"I'm always amazed at the stupidity some people displayed on the Internet," I said. "You carry a burner phone?"

"When I need one," she said. "I thought you might use carrier pigeons to communicate?" She wrinkled her nose and grinned.

"That the best you can do? I believe, Chief Laura Bright, you do have a small bit of humor." She ignored the comeback.

"I had scrounged social media and read posts by an amateur who blogs about cold cases," she said.

"He does what?" The incredulous look on Laura's face made me laugh.

"Touché, Robert Snow."

"My humor is dry and rare, but it does exist," I said.

"I'll tell Sam to issue you a department cell. Anyway, this man goes by the name of Jason Freeze. He publicizes unsolved cases on a true crime blog, The Freeze Report."

"How did he get interested in Marilyn Todd?"

"Don't you read the papers? His interest was pricked with the copycat theories to the Lyle murders that were in the editorials," Laura said.

"Thelma Burke's articles in The Bugle," I said.

"So, you have read them?"

"Just the Bugle. She didn't miss any opportunity to drag my name through the mud; announcing my guilt to the public. They are serious believers that I killed Marilyn, a copycat of Thomas Lyle and his two sons who were beaten to death in their sleep back in 1930," I said. "What about the curse? I'm not anywhere near a relative of the Lyle's."

"Do you believe in curses, Robert?" Bright asked.

"Nope. Just urban legends."

She continued, "It makes for a good tale to bring in some tourists. The ghost tour is popular. Nevertheless, as a tourist town we're not a heavy weight, like Gatlinburg and Pigeon Forge. People do not flock to Winfield Creek unless they are explorers or hikers. Our key revenue does not generate from the tourist trade. Most folks who live here are happy it doesn't. Too many strangers nosing around."

I replied, "I bet the town Aldermen and the Mayor did have the interest to build up a tourist trade. Keeping this murder story in the papers will do the trick."

Laura said, "Marilyn Todd beaten to death in her sleep makes a good story for the copycat theory. It makes my department look bad when we can't solve the case."

"Some people have a morbid need to feed on fear," I said.

"Wow, philosophical too," Laura said. At least, her tone was playful.

"I'm glad you're having fun, at my expense," I said.

Laura continued, "Some authors visit Winfield Creek for research on the Lyle family. Some are still trying to prove Timothy Lyle's death was murder. Others theorize who killed Thomas Lyle and his sons."

"When I move to a new place, I like to read up on its history. I have read about old man Timothy. He went missing for a couple of weeks and they found him on the side of a mountain. His head had been caved in and his spine broken."

"And missing his liver," Laura said. "People feared Spear-Finger killed him."

"Spear-Finger," I roared. "What kind of joke is that?"

"You didn't dig deep enough in your research. It's a Cherokee legend, a monster woman who lived high in the mountains. She fed on human livers. A shape-shifter, she had a stone spear-like finger. She used her finger to carve out her victim's liver."

"You don't believe that story, Laura." I looked over at her stoic face, "Do you?"

She laughed, "Murder comes in all shades. He had enemies. Timothy's anger was legendary. He was a hard man with a bad temper. Timothy married a Cherokee woman and during the removal, he faced stiff prejudice from settlers. Plenty of people know more than I do about their history. They say Timothy had never lost a fight; either with a fist, gun, or knife."

"He lost one fight, but it's a real long stretch to connect Timothy Lyle's death to Marilyn's murder," I said.

"The way her head is battered, no weapon found, no evidence and no suspects. Similar to the Thomas Lyle murders too," Laura said.

"Except, I'm one of two suspects in Marilyn's murder, and many in this town and elsewhere would like to see me locked up and convicted," I said.

"If it gives you any comfort, I don't consider you a suspect. Just a person of interest," Laura said.

"That makes me feel better, a little. When did you come to that conclusion?"

"I'm good at reading people; even in light of the Fort Meade case."

"No one could believe Ted Bundy had murdered those girls either," I said.

"From what I remember, he had a personality, and everyone close to him liked him."

"You're saying I don't have a personality."

"I'm saying many people don't like you, Robert. Besides, The Chief of Police controls who the suspects are and not the town residents."

"Your detective doesn't like me."

"Proves my point. Sam answers to me. Satisfied?"

"Do you like me?" I said.

"You're difficult. Do you require everyone to like you?"

"Nope," I said.

"I don't believe you're a cold-blooded murderer, but I don't trust you either." She smiled. I gave her my best sad expression.

I decided to change the subject. "Old man Timothy's bones could render some clues. We could have his body exhumed and examined. Forensics may shed some light on how he died. That also goes for Thomas and his sons."

"Many have tried to have Timothy's remains exhumed and had been turned down by the courts every time. He is a folk icon around here. There is not a judge in the county that will sign-off to dig him up. It's possible we can extrapolate a line of reasoning for the bodies of Thomas and his boys, but it's a long shot. By the way, where we are going?" Laura's cell rang.

"Hello, Mr. Raine," Laura said.

I drove and listened. Raine was the supervisor on TBI's forensic team investigation. Laura wrote in her notebook while she listened. When she clicked off her cell, she said, "Raine gave me the highlights of the lab report. The crime scene scrubbed clean. No evidence, DNA or otherwise, he said. Their air sniffer did pick up microbes that contained sandalwood oil. Nothing else."

"What's that mean?"

"Sandalwood oil is an ingredient in some perfumes and male shaving products. The fragrance in Marilyn's house didn't contain sandalwood." Laura tapped her iPhone. "Says here the sandalwood plant is protected because of over-harvesting."

"Does that make it expensive?" I pondered aloud.

"Raine said the autopsy report mentioned a small amount of Sandalwood paste found in the center of her forehead. According to Wikipedia, Sandalwood paste is used in religious rituals and applied to a devotee's foreheads, neck, or chest."

"Which religions used the paste?" I asked.

"Hinduism, Buddhism, and Islam in the Sufi sect, where the paste is applied to a devotee's grave. Information at our fingertips, what would we do without the Internet?"

"Go to the library," I said. Laura shook her head and continued reading her notes aloud. "The blood splatter on the wall was contaminated with strands of horsehair. The pattern wasn't consistent with one from a blunt instrument."

"He used a paint brush to splatter her blood?" I asked.

"Yes, the killer masked the natural pattern caused by the blows to Marilyn's head with the weapon?

"Why? It's obvious the killer used some kind of blunt instrument. He had another reason. Also, where would the paintbrush be hidden?"

"Or she had another reason," Laura amended. "The autopsy also found fragments of limestone in Todd's head and face wounds."

"I told you, a blunt instrument. The killer beat her to death with a rock. This mystery gets better and better."

"Maybe Spear-Finger did it." We both laughed out-loud to ease the tension. When she stopped laughing, Laura said, "Marilyn was eight weeks pregnant, with twins." My head snapped right.

"Keep your eyes on the road." A car horn blared. Tires squealed. I jolted and turned the wheel. The Explorer slid to a stop in the grass, inches from going over a bank. Our eyes locked, breathing hard.

"You okay?"

"I can see the headlines now. Chief Bright killed in a head-on collision, a passenger in the SUV of suspected killer, Robert Snow." She clamped her fist on the handgrip above the door.

"It could be worse. You may had survived the crash and then had to explain to the press your involvement with the suspected killer." I felt a nervous chill.

I guided the Explorer back on the road, and before Laura turned back to her notes on the autopsy findings, she said, "The press will have a field day when they find out about Marilyn's pregnancy, with twins. It's another connection with Thomas Lyle."

"I still don't buy this was a copycat murder," I said.

"Traces of Valium were found in her system, some undigested food, no alcohol."

"She didn't drink," I said.

"She needed a sedative after your date?" I let the jab pass. "You still haven't told me where we're going, Robert."

"We're going to see a little ole lady. Thelma Burke."

"You're going the wrong way. Thelma lives on Little Bear, the same block where Todd lived."

"Yes she does, but right now Thelma is at her mountain cabin over in Weirs Valley. Thelma called the police the morning I went to Marilyn's house. She is also the person who led the scared citizens to the mayor's office to proclaim me as public enemy number one, and she is blasting me in her editorials. She's writing a book about me as we speak."

Laura laughed, "You going to shake down a helpless old lady?"

"You think this is funny? I just want to ask her a few questions. She's a writer. They like to talk." Looking straight ahead, Laura settled back.

"Let's stop to eat before we get there," she said, "It's going to be a long day."

Chapter 13

Thelma Burke was a widow and author of crime fiction novels, in which her villains were serial killers. Three of her murder books were nonfiction, about the Lyle family.

After we had left the small diner, the ride to Thelma's cabin was a forty-five-minute drive up a narrow mountain road. Our maximum speed reached twelve miles per hour, except in the hairpin turns where we crawled slower than a snail.

We arrived at the small cabin that was near the mountaintop. Thelma was in her garden picking blueberries.

"She looks surprised to see us," Laura said.

"She is," I replied.

"Bad manners to show up unannounced," Laura said.

"You learn more when you arrive unannounced."

"I know, but it may not work with Thelma. She's a stickler for etiquette."

"Don't worry; I will be so polite you won't recognize me." We stepped out and stopped at the front of the Explorer. We waited. "She knows everything that happens in Winfield Creek. We can't ignore her."

"I know that," Laura whispered and stepped forward. "Good afternoon, Thelma," Laura said.

"Chief Bright, what brings you up here?" Thelma said walking towards us with a full pail of blueberries. She looked perturbed.

I put my best smile on. "We would like to ask you a few questions about the Marilyn Todd murder."

"Seems to me," Thelma paused to look at Laura," you're not the police, Mr. Snow, but you are the suspect."

"Mr. Snow is a person of interest. He's an experienced investigator and has agreed to help us with this case," Laura said.

"Well, he's the last known person to have seen her alive. The newspapers and many individuals in town and across the state, I might add, share my views. I know quite a bit about you, Mr. Snow."

"Robert," I said.

"First name implies we are on a friendly basis. I don't think so," Thelma said. "However, seeing as how you drove Chief Bright all the way up here, and she has vouched for your presence, you might as well come on inside." She motioned us inside the two-room cabin with a loft. It was roomier than it looked from the outside.

"I will put a kettle on for tea. Then you can ask your questions, Chief. Mind you though, I'm under no obligation to answer any that may incriminate me." I looked at Laura. Thelma's comment to invoke the Fifth Amendment had surprised her too. Her formal demeanor made it hard to tell if she was pulling our legs.

"This cabin had always been my husband's favorite place away from home," said Thelma from the open kitchen area. "I like it because it's quiet; a sanctuary where I can craft my stories without interruption. While the old man lived, we came up here every weekend, even in the winter. He liked to hunt and take long hikes. In the evening, we sat out there, by the garden, and watched the stars until morning. I miss him a great deal. Marilyn said her husband died a war hero, in Iraq." Thelma filled our cups then put the teapot on the polished cedar table. "Milk, and Honey?"

"Not for me," I said. Laura preferred sugar in her tea, and we waited while Thelma finished and handed us the cups. Then we settled back in the cushioned chairs.

"Marilyn did not like to entertain visitors in her home. She worked hard to be invisible in plain sight. I suppose, she came to Winfield Creek to be left alone." Thelma said.

"Did Marilyn tell you that?" I said.

"No, it was my observation, Mr. Snow. I made it a point to befriend to her, as I do with a lot of folks," Thelma said. "People trust me and I'm a good listener." She raised her teacup, sipped, and then added, "There were things she kept hidden."

"What kind of things?" Laura asked.

"She was pregnant." Thelma paused to gauge our reaction.

"We know, twins," said Laura. Thelma was surprised, and she tried not to let it show, but her facial expression gave her away. Then Thelma composed her thoughts. "Marilyn talked about her husband, but expressed little emotion, it was as though she read from a prepared script. My late husband served in World War II, Korea and in the early years of Vietnam. Wounded in action twice and each time my emotions were on edge," her voice crackled. She pulled a handkerchief from her pocket and dabbed her eyes. "He retired a Major General," she continued. "Nevertheless, I questioned Marilyn on a few things Army wives tend to know, and Marilyn didn't have a clue."

Laura went straight to the point, "Thelma, think back to the day of the murder. Did you see or hear anything, out of the ordinary that morning?"

"Marilyn didn't like small talk unless she initiated it." Thelma sipped her tea. *Why did she dodge Laura's question?* I wondered. We waited and then Thelma said, "I gave my statement to the detective who canvassed the hood."

"The hood?" Laura and I said at the same time.

"I study slang. I'm a writer, you know," she said with a demeaning tone. "I have been waiting for the right moment to use that word. You found it funny. Is it because of my age? Well at seventy-five, I can still learn new things. Do not much care for the new music though. My late husband was older. I had just turned thirteen when we eloped. Jailbait, but that did not stop us. Sound asleep at the hour Marilyn died." *Finally, she answered the damn question.* Laura looked over, and I took the cue.

"Some people theorized Marilyn's murder was a copycat of the Thomas Lyle case. What's your opinion, Mrs. Burke?" Thelma looked to Laura for her approval before she answered.

"I'm certain it was. I am an expert on the Lyle family. My belief is a member of the Lyle family murdered Thomas and his sons. The one who carried the Cain gene killed them. The family is cursed."

"So I've heard," I replied. "Then you believe in the curse?"

"What I accept Mr. Snow is that the family has an evil element in its gene pool that drives them to commit murder, and they are unable to control it," Thelma said.

"That's also a description of a psychopath. Until Marilyn, there have been no killings like this," I said.

"Serial killers can operate undetected for years. Maybe there are undiscovered bodies buried all over Winfield Creek, but they don't have to be in Winfield Creek either," Thelma countered.

"Do you have any theories why someone targeted Marilyn?" I said.

"No," Thelma replied. "No apparent motive, just like Thomas and his sons. Nothing in the stories about the curse indicated the killer's victims were exclusive to the Lyle family."

I pondered that thought and sipped tea. Thelma broke the silence, "Thomas Lyle had twin boys. The killer wants the police to think this is a copycat murder, for whatever reason I could not guess, Mr. Snow."

"No forced entry, Marilyn had opened the door for the killer. She knew and trusted the person who had killed her," Laura said.

Twisting in her seat, Thelma lifted her teacup to her lips. "Oh," Thelma said, and then she added, "That doesn't leave Mr. Snow off the hook." She sipped more tea and peered at me over her cup, proud she had established the connection.

"Nor does it exclude several other folks either," Laura said.

"My curiosity peaked with Marilyn's manner," Thelma said. "She was not genuine. A woman who can talk about her husband's death with no emotion is off-kilter, in my opinion."

"I know people who can express tragedy and not shed a tear," I said.

"Nevertheless, if she lost her husband to the war, her distress should have been evident. I've had the belief he was an imaginary spouse."

"Never thought of that," Laura said.

"Imaginary, you mean like she had a mental problem?" I said.

"A crime writer examines how people react to every conceivable situation. Marilyn was smart. I believe she concocted the story about her husband."

"Why would Marilyn fabricate a spouse who had been killed in the war?" I said.

"That's an excellent question to ponder, and there are many reasons. For one, it gives her instant sympathy and credibility in a small town with conservative and patriotic residents. People have a tendency to be sensitive towards widows," Thelma said.

"This is the Bible belt where many are less sensitive to an unwed mother," Laura said. "And besides, if what you suspect is true, the father may not know he's their father."

"Or he may know and doesn't like it," I said. "Wouldn't be the first pregnant woman murdered by her lover."

"My, my, things are getting interesting," Thelma quipped.

"This is a quandary, Mrs. Burke; you said that Marilyn didn't know things that Army wives should be aware," I said. "Please elaborate."

"Several, she didn't know anything about rank, MOS or the lifestyle of a military family. In the time we talked, Marilyn never used her husband's name. She scripted her story. A woman, who is pretending to be someone else, should have done some research about the military. That's why she couldn't convince me that she had a husband."

"She may have been forced to concoct the cover story on the fly. The one date I had with her she didn't tell me anything other than her reason to escape the big city life," I said.

"Mr. Snow, you're a man. You were enthralled with Marilyn's beauty. You really think she would have told you about her husband. The only thing on your mind was getting her in bed." My face flushed with anger. Thelma's smug smile made it worse. Laura spoke before I could get my words out.

"How long will you be up here, Thelma?" Laura said.

"I will be back in town next week." Thelma kept her eyes on mine, proud that she had gotten to me.

"Will that be a Monday or Tuesday? We may have more questions, to pick your brain so to speak."

"Come on Thursday. I have an appointment on Friday," Thelma said.

"That will be just fine," Laura said.

Thelma looked me dead in the eye, "In my book, Mr. Snow, the finger of suspicion is pointed at you."

We left, anger still boiled in my gut. We walked across the small front yard toward the Explorer. "That woman really torqued me," I said to Laura.

"I could tell."

"She was evasive and snobbish; a real know-it-all."

"It was a figure of speech, or maybe a .finger. of speech, Robert."

"Ha, ha, smart aleck," I said.

"Like you said before, she likes to talk. She's opinionated," Laura said.

"She writes fiction. That makes her a professional liar," I said.

Chapter 14

A week after Marilyn's death, I decided a change of scenery was in order. It was a good day to keep my promise to Charley, to scope out his son, David. More importantly, I needed to observe the woman he had befriended. It was an easy task, and the drive over to Knoxville provided time to relieve some anxiety from the Todd case.

The stress kicked my regular sleep pattern all to hell, and my temperament was on the ragged edge. This case had monopolized all my time, leaving no opportunities to visit Angry Rock.

The Knoxville traffic was light on Fifth Avenue. David's Firebird was parked along the curb across the street from the Fifth Ave apartments. I guided the Explorer into a parking space two cars back from David's and settled in for an ordinary stakeout.

When I was eating the second pack of peanut butter crackers, David with the woman emerged from the apartment building and walked across the street. My Winfield Creek Police-issued cell phone vibrated, "Hello," I answered.

A male voice said, "A warning. You do not want to pursue these people."

"With whom am I speaking?" I said.

"You need to shut up and listen. These two are beyond your reach, Bob. Drop it. Mind your own business. Stick to what you know, and live out your retirement."

"These two people happen to be the business of a friend, making it my business. The woman you killed was my friend. It's personal," I said.

"I'm not her killer, but I may be yours." The caller hung up.

Before I had time to ponder the threat, David, and his bald girlfriend zoomed off in the Firebird. Charley was right. She was much older than David was. Wearing a sleeveless shirt and shorts, the tattoos stood out on her arms and legs. Her height and build put her close to Mason Dew's description of the woman running from Marilyn's house. She had shaved off her hair to change her appearance.

David turned onto Magnolia toward downtown. After a thirty-five minute drive winding through a few side streets, he entered the State

Street parking garage parking garage. I drove past the Firebird and parked. I walked close behind them for a while. They did not suspect I was tailing, but I couldn't afford to be careless either. If the tattooed woman were the killer, she would be on alert.

I followed them to Market Square. The July heat and humidity was brutal. A farmers' market was set up, and it was crowded. It was a challenge to keep the pair in sight and at the same time, watch my six. It was not a smart move to shrug off the threat, and the man who phoned it may have been close. I thought, *Why would he want to scare me off these two?*

I didn't spot anyone following us when we drove over from the apartments. Nonetheless, either the man was a pro, or he knew our destination and took a different route. My focus was David and the woman. I couldn't let the threat on my life interfere with the task. *Stay vigilant and respond to the situation,* I told myself. It was not the ideal plan, but it was all I had. While David's woman browsed at the first farm vendor's table, I stopped at an art display and pretended to be interested in a watercolor.

David was on edge. He kept watching the crowd flow by as though he was looking for someone. While I waited, my thoughts drifted to the phone call. It wasn't Mason Dew. I would have recognized his meek voice. This man had a distinctive diction and professional tone. It may have been the man who I fought in Marilyn's house, but I wasn't sure because he hadn't spoken while he kicked my ass.

"That's a beautiful watercolor of Siler's Bald," a female voice interrupted my thoughts.

"Yes, it is beautiful," I said.

"Two hundred and fifty dollars, if you're interested. I can box it for you. We accept all credit cards."

"Just admiring, thank you," I said and moved on. David's tattooed woman held up a cucumber and bargained with the proprietor, while David scanned the crowd of people that milled up and down the street. He was definitely watching out for someone. I wondered if it was someone they were meeting here or somebody they wanted to avoid. By the intent look on his face, the latter seemed more plausible.

The proprietor turned away from David's woman to help someone else. David tapped her arm to draw her attention to the modern sculptor inside a small park on the other side of the mall. A man was watching David. He was lean and close to six feet tall, dressed in a Tennessee orange tee shirt, matching shorts, a ball cap, and sneakers. He had an empty shopping bag folded under his arm. He looked ordinary.

David pulled his tattooed woman away from the stand. They hit a fast stride weaving in and out of the crowd. I followed from a comfortable distance, the stranger increased speed to close the gap on David. This was an unfamiliar place. Tracking David, watching the goon, and reading the street sign at the same time was difficult.

The woman held onto David's hand, her head swiveled trying to locate the pursuer. We left Market Square onto a connected street. Vendors lined both sides making the road a narrow tightly packed lane of people. The slow milling crowd made it harder to keep David in uninterrupted view. The man pursuing them had the same difficulty, like a salmon swimming upstream.

An old lady with a dog on a leash impeded my movement. The delay was enough to lose sight of David, and the unknown man who was in pursuit had vanished.

Hot and sweaty, I stood and turned in a circle observing the crowd for any sign of David. It took a few minutes, but I spotted him. He and the woman were on the sidewalk at Summer Place, walking behind the vendors' stands. Using the vendor's as cover they were doubling back towards the Oliver Hotel.

I walked, staying behind and parallel to their position. I didn't see the other man, but my instincts told me he was close. We were back on the Mall moving in the direction of the Tennessee Valley Authority towers. David used the crowd and the vendors' tents as shields. They turned right and walked behind the performance stage in the direction that would take them down the hill to Gay Street.

"There they are!" A loud voice screamed. The proprietor, from the vegetable stand where David's girlfriend had held up the cucumber, ran towards them with a policewoman in tow. David's head turned from side to side. He's conflicted. Run or stop? He stopped.

Apparently, he figured the police was a better option than dealing with the other man pursuing them. *Who was that guy whom David feared?*

I kept my eye on David while the policewoman questioned his woman. Then I moved past the wet pavement where barefoot children darted in and out of waterspouts to cool off in the summer heat.

Near the performance stage, I strolled into the gathering of curious onlookers watching the police activity and then I saw the man. He looked directly at me, smiled and then he disappeared into the crowd.

David and his bald girlfriend argued with the proprietor. Two other police officers arrived and spent a few minutes talking with David's woman. They were more interested in her than what she had in the shopping bag. The proprietor was still shouting while the policewoman started to move the bystanders back. One cop handcuffed David's girlfriend. Then other was in a struggle with David.

I clicked on the cell and speed dialed Laura's number. Charley needed to know what had happened to his son, and Laura was the best person to break the news to him. Charley did not deserve the added burden he had enough with his wife's illness.

Chapter 15

The return drive to the Creek gave me time to analyze the situation. David was living with a suspected murderess. *Is he an accomplice or a stooge?* For now, I chose to believe the latter. I didn't want to accept Charley's boy would be involved with murder, but I knew that bad things happened to good families too.

Death threats were not a new business for me. I added this one to a long list. A bigger concern was how he got the department-issued cell phone number. By the time I arrived at the station, Laura had the transfer order completed. David and his companion were in the Winfield Creek lockup. Charley was in the interrogation room pacing from one end to the other. I strolled over to Reynolds' desk.

"Detective"

"What do you want, Agent Man?" he said without looking up.

"I'm retired CID, remember, and it was Special Agent."

"Heard you're getting your Private Investigator license," Reynolds snickered without looking up from his laptop.

"I received a call on this department-issued cell and I wondered how he got the number?" I said, ignoring Reynolds' jab.

Reynolds stopped typing, looked up, and said, "A guy called, said he and you were old Army buddies, and wanted to get in touch. I gave him the number." Reynolds smirked and turned back to his report.

"This was supposed to be a secure number, Detective." Reynolds ignored the lecture with a grunt, and I turned away wondering how this goofball became a detective.

"I figured if you two were in cahoots, I could get you both locked up eventually. Worth a shot. Unfortunately, he blocks his calls."

"Nice work," Laura said when I opened her office door.

"I didn't do much."

"Try to give a guy credit—anyway looks like we have our killer. That counts for something," she said.

"It gets Burke off my back and the mayor off yours. That counts for a lot. Why is Charley in the interrogation room?" I asked.

"He needed a quiet place to think."

"Maybe we have the killer and maybe we don't," I said.

"You have that look."

"What look?"

"You furrow your eyebrows whenever you're unsure of something," she said.

"No one has ever told me that before."

"Just don't play poker, Robert."

"Anyone pick up Mason Dew yet?"

"He skipped town. The clerk said he paid his bill and left the day after your visit. You must have scared him."

"We need him to identify the woman," I said.

"That's a statement from Captain Obvious," said Laura. "Sam is coordinating with the Park Rangers and a couple of my officers will assist them. Dew has a day head start."

"If your officers can keep pace with the park rangers, they should be able to find Dew. That is if he is on the mountain. Like I said before, he's not a long-distance hiker."

"We have to rule it out. Where else would he have gone?"

"We'll know when we find him," I said with a smirk. Laura threw her hands up.

"Can Charley stay with you a couple of days?" Laura inquired, switching topics. "He needs a friend. Not easy when you find out your son is mixed up with a murderess."

"I'm puzzled about something else—you had an APB out on the woman. Those tattoos make her stand out in a crowd. She shacked up with Charley's son in a part of Knoxville that gets a lot of police attention. Why didn't she get picked up before now?"

"Hiding in plain sight," said Laura, "The oldest game in the book."

"Did you issue the APB?"

"No, Sam did. Why?" Laura asked.

"The APB was issued before we knew about her tattoos. I wonder if Reynolds updated the APB with the new information. A killer is hiding from the law and she's nabbed for shoplifting a cucumber."

"I'll take it anyway we can get it, as long as it's legal."

"What's her name?"

"Monica Love," Laura said.

"Ironic last name. How did you get her transferred so fast?"

"Knoxville had her on shoplifting. I told them I got her on murder one. I guess she got here quicker than you because the police don't drive like old men." She winked at me.

"We only got her if Dew identifies her," I said, ignoring the jab.

"He will," Laura said. "Although, the circumstances are not ideal. We don't have tangible evidence to tie Love to the murder. Just a half-baked witness, and if he falls through the cracks we're done. No murder weapon, no fingerprints, and no DNA to test against Love for a match. She will walk and I will look like a jackass."

"We will both look like jackasses. What's her motive? Did she lawyer up?" I asked.

"We haven't talked to her yet. Hoping the wait will rattle her nerves. So, we don't know her motive, but we will, and she hasn't requested her lawyer."

"She lived in a dive, her clothes are from the eighties, and she doesn't have the big bucks. A public defender will be the best she gets. Put the pressure on her, Laura. Also, there was a man following them at Market Square, and they knew him; somehow, he is connected. We need her to tell us about him. I saw fear on David's face when he spotted the man. I can't say if Love was scared, but they moved fast to get away from him. When the police got involved, the man disappeared like a ghost." Before Laura could respond, O'Connor walked into the office and handed her a business card.

"Chief, Love had requested her phone call, and she asked for someone to contact her lawyer."

Laura looked at the card and whistled, "A woman who didn't have two nickels in her pocket, and she has an expensive lawyer." She handed me the card.

"Brooks, Nash, and Taylor," I said. "Are they good?"

"They are the best in the state. Nash handles criminal, and he doesn't lose," said Laura. "O'Connor, make the phone call. Take your time. I'm going to have a chat with Love." Laura gave the order, and then she left the office before I could tell her about the death threat.

Laura forced Charley to exit the interrogation room so she could use it to question Monica Love. He looked like a lost puppy. "Come on Charley," I said. "My place. I'll cook dinner and then we will figure out what we need to do next."

Chapter 16

I seared pork tenderloin in a deep pan. I removed the pork and pan-glazed onions, layered the pork on the onions, added 2 cups of broth, poured 1 cup of maple syrup over the pork. I sprinkled on rosemary, salt, pepper and then covered the pan.

"I'm glad you called me," Laura said. "Where have you been?"

"Charley and I spent a couple of days together like you asked."

"I'm glad you spent some time with him. Dinner smells great," she said. "You must be a good cook."

"Baked potato or rice?"

"Potato," she said.

"I'm a fair cook; a bachelor has to know the basics," I said. "The pork will cook for forty-five minutes. In the meantime, we can go over some of the reports." I refreshed her third glass of Chardonnay.

"Thanks. You're drinking root beer?"

"Have to keep my wits about me."

"Is it because the Chief of Police is having dinner at your place?"

"No, we are going through my notes on the Mary Rinehart case, and I need to be able to think straight. Besides, I quit drinking a year ago."

"Have a drinking problem?"

"Quit before it became one."

"Good move. You keep your wits. My drinking won't bother you?"

"I gave you the wine."

"Yes, you did. If you don't drink, why have the wine in the house?" Her warm breath felt good when she moved close.

"For special occasions, like this one," I managed to say. Laura's attention was not on the case files. "Am I too old for you?" I stammered.

"You have been around Winfield Creek. How many younger men have you seen in this town, Robert?"

"A few," I said. She leaned closer and spoke in a soft tone, "No one who is available and desirable." Between kisses she said, "Work can wait till morning."

Chapter 17

At four A.M., sleep was hard to come by. I needed my usual morning run before breakfast to clean out the cobwebs. I exited without waking Laura. Three hours later, I found Laura puttering around the kitchen. "Hey, Bob, have a good run?" she said holding the frying pan, "Thought I would cook breakfast."

"Great, I'll take a quick shower." I poured a cup of coffee before going to the bathroom.

"Hope you like your eggs scrambled."

"I do and the bacon crisp," I said, stepping into the hot shower.

After I had dried off, I threw on a pair of jeans and a t-shirt. "Not used to a woman in the kitchen. Breakfast looks delicious."

"Have a good run?" She said again while I spread homemade apple butter on my toast.

"Yeah, I need to keep in shape." Small talk. We were compensating for an awkward moment: the morning after. Making love to the Chief of Police had been unexpected. "It's been a while for me," I blurted out.

"I would not have guessed, Bob." I looked down feeling like a schoolboy. Laura said, "This is awkward for us, but I had a good time without regrets."

"I have no regrets, Laura."

"Good, no problems. A biological urge satisfied," she said. "Let's work on the Rinehart files after we eat."

"I'd like that," I said. "The Rinehart murder was my downfall. That and uncontrolled anger management forced early retirement. Pride wasn't easy to swallow."

Laura said, "We can work together to solve the Todd case, and then I will help you figure out the Rinehart case. Right now, we need to rule out any connections, other than you, to these two cases."

"You're consorting with a suspect. That may shorten your career."

"Not to mention my soiled reputation. My eyes are wide open, Mr. Snow," she said in a playful tone.

"Being suspected of murder was not how I planned to spend retirement. I can't complain about the treatment from the Chief of

Police though." We had a good laugh. "I'll brew more coffee."

"Tell me more about Mary."

"Mary was a sweet and kind soul, like Marilyn."

"They were alike in other ways too," Laura said. "You met Marilyn at the Grinder. Who initiated the contact?"

"She came over to my table and introduced herself. She knew I was new in town, Newcomers, she had called us."

I poured fresh coffee in Laura's cup. "And Mary, how did you meet her?" Laura looked over her coffee cup with her penetrating eyes. *She can see right through me*, I thought.

"Mary worked at the 1st Army Headquarters, and my office was a few blocks away. We met when she had almost plowed into my car at the PX parking lot. A beautiful woman with a full smile, we hit it off right away. I had a house on base, and she lived in Ridge Water. We dated a few times, and then I gave her a key to my place. She often came over before I got home from work and cooked dinner. The last time I saw her, I arrived home and found her on the couch, dead, a bullet hole through her head." Laura put her hand on mine. "Mary and I were good friends. She had her career, and I had mine. Love and a long term relationship were never in the conversation."

"You're a bachelor. How did you get on-base housing?" Laura asked.

"Connections," I replied.

"How long were you and Mary dating?"

"A few months," I said. "She was in the wrong place at the wrong time. The intruder ransacked the house, but nothing was stolen. My opinion then, and still is, the house had been turned upside down to make it look like a break-in gone wrong."

"I take it that was a minority opinion," Laura said.

"After some dead ends and no real evidence, the case went cold. I couldn't leave it alone and my workload suffered."

"Robert, what caliber of weapon did the gunman use?"

"Forty-five. I carried a 45 Commander, and whispers of a domestic dispute started to circulate the office."

"They checked your weapon, didn't they?" Laura said.

"Ballistics cleared me. It remained office gossip. Couldn't drop it and every minute on and off duty I spent looking for the killer. That's why my superior got on my back, and in a heated moment, he accused me of botching the case to cover my tracks."

"That's when you slugged him," Laura said. "And he gave you

the option to retire to avoid a court martial."
"Like I said, at one time we had been friends."
"Maybe not," Laura said.

Chapter 18

I pushed hard and reached the ridge in record time. My muscles burned, and sweat rolled down my body like rain. I climbed the six-foot side of Angry Rock, stripped off my clothes, and stood at the edge. The slight breeze caressed tight muscles. Stretching I leaned forward and looked over the edge. Two hundred feet down to the narrow stream that snaked through the valley floor. In the distance, new homes were going up every day on the mountain, a blight that destroyed the wilderness. A deep male voice startled me. "Good morning, Special Agent Snow."

I turned half way around. The voice belonged to a thin well-built man, dressed in sweats, who stood twenty feet away at the trailhead. He was breathing heavy, and he held a Glock in his right hand.

"I don't have any money on me. No drugs either."

"I could have shot you without saying a word," he said. "Your body would have tumbled over the edge. The buzzards, insects, and other wildlife would feast on your flesh."

"You didn't mention the coyotes that would gnaw on my bones. Who are you and how do you know me?" I said.

"Everyone around here knows Robert Snow," the man chuckled. "Suspected killer who also is the lover of the Chief of Police. Nice move Bob."

"Still don't know your name."

"Jack Cree," he said.

"Never heard of you," I said.

"Bob, I'm disappointed you don't remember me." A wide menacing grin spanned his mouth. I wanted to punch his face.

"Why should I remember someone I had never met?" I did recognize the man; in Knoxville, he had chased David and Monica.

"Bob, just the other day in Knoxville. Have you forgotten so soon?"

"Why did you follow me?"

"How is the head, Bob? You're keeping your body in good shape for a retired guy."

"You're admiring my assets?"

"Don't worry, I'm straight," he said.

"I'm not worried, just curious," I said.

"Climb down and dress, and keep your hands out in the open. You're in great running shape, but your jujitsu is a little rusty, Bob."

"You're the guy with the hard drive," I said. "Why did you take it? Why did you kill Marilyn Todd, and why did you go after David Farber?"

"Whoa, slow down, Bob. So many questions; first, yes I hit you with the hard drive; second, I did not kill Todd and third; my business with the punk kid is personal. My employer specified to get the drive, not burn a copy. Todd had not been my target, but we can chit-chat later when we get back to your house," Cree said.

"I'd love to wipe that grin off your face."

"Come down nice and slow."

I climbed down from the rock while sizing him up to formulate a plan and escape this situation.

"Nam," he said.

"Nam, that was a long time ago. A faded memory," I said.

"I had a few changes made to my face since then. In my business, staying the same equals getting dead fast. Here is a hint: Lieutenant Colbert."

"Colbert was a boyhood friend, murdered, the crime scene rigged to make his death look like a suicide," I said.

"See you do remember, Bob. You were the one who did not buy the suicide. You stuck your nose in where it did not belong. You were a grunt back then, and you went off on your own tirade. You didn't know when to quit, even though all of the evidence pointed to suicide," Cree said.

"It's why I got into CID."

"You still did not prove that case wasn't suicide. Your constant digging made important people in high places nervous. They wouldn't sanction a hit on a special agent in CID. The next best option was to take out someone you loved. Mary Rinehart paid the price for your stupidity. Your record of accomplishment on a whole was good, but you never did get it with Colbert or Rinehart. What makes you think you're going to do any better with the Todd case?"

"I still don't place you," I said trying hard to control my anger.

"I piloted Colbert's chopper. He did not know I worked for Military Intelligence. You and I had met once, at Camp Evans. It is extraordinary how a few surgical alterations around the eyes, nose, and a different hair color changed my looks. I took Colbert out on my first contract. These days, I contract to several agencies."

"Why did you kill him?"

"It doesn't matter why Bob. Now you know you were right all along. That should make you feel better about yourself." Cree's words stung like a hornet.

"I still think you killed Marilyn," I said.

"There is so much you need to know, Bob. Take the point down the trail," Cree said using the Glock like a pointer.

"How did Chief Bright stack up with Mary? In bed, I mean." I remained quiet, and Cree continued to talk. "The number one suspect beds the Chief of Police. Now that was a sweet move." My fingers pressed the waistband of my shorts where my shiv was stowed in a small pouch. A crude blade but useful in close quarter combat. Against a pro like Cree, the odds of getting the element of surprise were next to zero. Nevertheless, this guy deserved some serious payback and the only way to get the upper hand would be to make my move before we reached the house.

Scenarios raced through my brain; the way to survive against his weapon would be to get off this path and get Cree into the brush. His huffing and puffing meant Cree couldn't handle the humidity. In the thick woods on the mountain, I had the advantage.

"You're quiet, Bob. You are scheming up an escape plan. It's the first thing a captured soldier does."

"Why didn't you just shoot me, Jack? Or was a mock suicide your plan?"

"That would be interesting, Bob. Your death comes later," Cree said. "It will be beautiful and clean, poetic. For instance, the Army and FBI received evidence that Lieutenant Colbert did not kill himself after all. The killer happened to be his friend Master Sergeant Robert Snow," Cree said with a snide chuckle. "You were a dud, Bob. How did you manage to get into the CID and with a Warrant Officer grade?"

"How will you frame me for a murder you committed, Jack? There's no evidence, remember?"

"Incriminating evidence can be manufactured by someone who is gifted in such matters. I have proof connecting you to the Colbert and Rinehart murders. I could throw in the Todd death for an extra bonus if I wanted. Evidence packaged and labeled like it came from a serial killer's trophy collection."

"You must hate me to go to all of that trouble, Cree."

"I don't hate you, Bob. I made a promise to myself that if given the opportunity I would get even for the trouble you stirred up over Colbert. You're not in CID anymore. You're nobody."

"Then kill me and get it over with," I chided.

"Too easy," Cree chuckled. "No satisfaction."

"Why did you wait for all of those years?" I kept Cree talking.

"I returned to the states processed out of MI. You would be surprised how much civilian work is available for a person with exceptional talent and few morals."

"Few morals? I don't think you have any."

"The pay was exceptional. I kept busy and you were put on hold." While Cree was bantering about himself, I faked a stumble on a tree root, going down to one knee.

"I sprained my ankle."

"Pity. Get up. I know you're tougher than a little sprain," he said. Turning to shield the shiv retrieved from the waistband, I said,

"Give me a second before we go on."

"Not in your life, Bob," Cree said and then shoved me with his foot. He kept the Glock aimed at my head. The shove pushed me over, and my left hand came around with the shiv and sliced at Cree's leg. I rolled down the steep slope. Jack double-timed. "You did not cut flesh, Snow!" he shouted.

Where the path turned, I splayed my legs to stop rolling, jumped up, and bolted between the trees and through the brush. The report from the unsilenced Glock echoed across the mountain. *No one will be alarmed; people shoot guns up here all the time.*

I ran fast and put distance between us, over rocky ground and protruding tree roots. I flung my arms to sweep back the branches that hung at face level. Cree had kicked my ass at Marilyn's house, but he was on my turf now. Limbs cracked and brush rustled behind and to the right. Jack was running across the slope, on a parallel line, trying to out-distance and intercept. He would not win. Cree had shot once and missed. He would not fire again until he had a clear shot. I knew about a shallow cave a hundred yards ahead, a good place to set an ambush. He had to come down the slope to catch me, and then I would spring the trap.

After thirty minutes in the cave, Cree had not arrived. If he was still in pursuit, he had gone quiet or dropped dead from exhaustion, "too much to hope for," I mumbled.

Chapter 19

Another thirty minutes passed without a sound from Cree. I climbed out of hiding and crawled up the slope, looking in all directions. Without a sign of Cree, I wondered if he had withdrawn. I went back toward the house, looking for any sign where Cree could be waiting to spring an ambush.

Within fifteen yards from the house and no sign of Cree, I figured he was inside waiting for me to waltz through the door. The Explorer was the lone vehicle in the driveway. Cree must have parked further down the road. "Cree, come on out," I yelled and received no response.

I stayed small and trotted toward the house. Stopping on the left side, planted my back against the cedar siding, and looked in the guest bedroom window. Clear. I moved along the side to the master bedroom window. The window blind obstructed my view into the room. I didn't remember if I had pulled the blind down this morning.

I continued to the front and peered through the living room window. Clear. I made a mental note to get opaque drapes, and then examined the front door. There was no sign of forced entry. Crouched below the windows, I moved to the right side and then to the back porch. I turned over the rock in the flower bed. The spare key was gone. Slow and quiet, I stepped across the wood porch to the kitchen door. With the shiv clenched between my teeth, I turned the doorknob and pushed on the door, dropped and rolled into the kitchen. I stopped alongside the bar with a thump.

The fresh air in the house began to exchange with the hot, humid air outside. Cree had to know I was in. The logical action for Cree was to attack. *What is he waiting for?*

It 'd be good to have the 45, but it was stored in the secretary by the front door. The quiet house was unnerving. I sneaked a quick look around the corner of the bar. The hallway between the bedrooms was clear.

That left the bathroom and the master bedroom. I expected Cree to have taken a position in the master. That's where I would be, behind the bed. There was a small chance he was in the bathroom. "Take nothing for granted," I whispered, and then moved fast toward the bathroom door.

Heart pounding I stayed low, traversed the room at full speed, and struck the door leading with the left shoulder. The door flew open and the shiv sliced through the air as my right arm pushed out quick jabs searching for the target, the door slammed against the stop. The blade found no resistance. I lost my balance, fell through the shower curtains and into the tub.

My shoulder and ribs screamed pain. Somehow, I had the mental capacity to throw the shiv, or I would have stabbed myself. Embarrassed, I squirmed around in the bathtub to get on my back. I imagined Cree standing in the doorway, with his finger on the trigger, laughing.

"Get it together, Bob," I muttered. I stayed still for a time using the bathtub for cover in case Cree charged from the master. After five minutes, it was evident Cree was going to wait for me to open the door. I struggled to lift myself from the bathtub and made a mental note to have handicapped rails installed. I stood sideways in the hall. A metallic smell reached out from the master bedroom. The odor was faint. I crouched and then kicked the door open and rushed in.

Cree was not waiting for me. Monica Love's dead body lay on the bed, covered in blood and beaten to a pulp, like Marilyn.

Chapter 20

My cell chimed, I was turning the Explorer into the parking lot at the police station. Once again, the caller ID read 'Private Caller.' "Hello."

"They want me dead," the male voice said.

"Who is this?" I asked.

"I want to meet," the man said.

"Whoever this is, don't play games with me."

"Bob, can't you recognize my voice? It's Jack. Monica Love is an alias."

"I have no idea what you're talking about."

"Don't be specious, Bob. The dead body in your bed, she worked with me," Cree said. "I trained her."

"So, what's that to me? And I don't appreciate the mess you left me, Cree."

"I didn't kill her."

"Why are you asking to meet?" I said. "What about getting even with me? Or is screwing over your employer more fun?"

"You're a smart guy, Bob. You figured out I burned a copy of that hard drive. What can I say; curiosity got the best of me."

"More like greed," I said.

"Getting even with you, that's my ace in the hole," he chuckled. "I have the evidence tucked away in a safe place, and anything happens to me it gets sent to Justice. It's enough evidence to pin Colbert and Rinehart's deaths on you. That should give you the motivation to help me stay alive."

"You don't scare me," I said. "Your employer can have you for all I care, and I'll take my chances with the Justice Department."

"Like it or not we have something in common, Bob."

"Yeah, what's that, Jack?"

"We have the same enemies."

"How well did you know Todd?" I said.

"I didn't know her. My assignment was to retrieve the hard drive," Cree said.

"How long did you know Monica?"

"Years, Bob." Silence hung heavy in the air. I waited and then Cree said, "I loved her." He paused. "Do we have an agreement to meet?"

"I will meet with you." I paused. "I don't believe you have manufactured evidence to send to Justice. Therefore, here is my counter offer. Turn yourself in today, and I will escort you. You can pour your heart out to Chief Bright. We'll keep you under wraps; whoever they send can't find you." Cree laughed with a sarcastic tone.

"Bob, that is lame. You know damn well you cannot stop anyone the National Security Agency sent. No, we will not meet at that out-of-date police station. I will choose a safe place and call you when it's time," said Cree. "You and Laura, no one else or nobody walks away alive."

"No dice. Just me. Laura's out of it."

"On the contrary, Bob. She is up to her beautiful neck in this affair. You caused a ton of problems in Nam. Then you got yourself in CID. You just could not let Colbert go. You had to meddle, and you made famous people your enemies. You were good. Dangerous classified missions and you managed not to get yourself killed, much to the dismay of many influential people in key positions." Cree paused, for the effect I supposed.

I waited him out, and after a minute, he said, "You had talent, and you were a worthy adversary, but I need more from you. In return, I will give you inside information that will keep you occupied until you're eighty. As a bonus, I can give you what you have been searching for, the truth on Colbert."

"I'm retired."

"Yeah right," Cree said. "You have a gift for getting in the middle of the action. You work with me or suffer the loss of another lover and go to prison to boot." I didn't respond, but my blood boiled when Cree threatened Laura. Cree said, "I'll give you a little something more, to show my good faith. You are closer to Todd's killer than you think."

"Monica Love killed Todd, Jack."

"I know you don't believe that, and I know you saw through that so-called witness. I'll let you know the place and time for the meet." Jack hung up.

"Crap," I said into the disconnected phone. I walked through the station door, and the clerk waved me through the metal detector like a regular employee. Laura had an espresso and a honey bun waiting for me. After slugging down the espresso, I said, "Cree wants to meet."

"Wait—who?" I explained to her how I had met and escaped the man who had followed Monica Love and Charley's son.

"We had gotten an anonymous call about Love. I guess that was you. When did you speak to Cree?" She asked.

"Outside. He called my cell. Tried to find his number, but he used a burner phone."

"Why does he want to meet?" She probed.

"He crossed the National Security Agency. He copied files from the hard drive he stole from Marilyn's computer. The records on that drive must be vital. He said he would call with the time and the place. He will meet with me and you - no one else."

"This is getting weird," she said. "The NSA is involved. Who the hell does this Cree guy think he is?"

"He's a freelancer who believes he is invincible," I said.

"If we don't play ball, Cree's next hit is you." Laura's eyes widened, and she blew out a breath.

"He told you that?" She said.

"He did. I'm not going to let that happen. Cree said our killer is closer than we think. He knows who killed Todd and Love, and he said he will give me the truth about John Colbert."

"Cree wants to hang Colbert on you, and now he's going to tell you why it went down?"

"He will say why he killed Colbert and still try to hang me with it," I said.

"We have to do the meeting," said Laura. "In the meantime, I'll contact my friend at FBI for information on a Jack Cree."

"He's reliable?"

"He is a straight arrow and won't go against bureau policy. So if they have a classified book on Cree, we won't know."

"How close a friend is he?" I said.

"I hope you're not suggesting what I think you are." Her eyes narrowed. "Not that close. He is married with children." I dropped the subject and chewed on the honey bun.

"He has already told me the FBI has a file on Marilyn. Turns out, she showed up on an inter-agency alert. Marilyn worked for the NSA, and they accused her of stealing secret files. Marilyn Todd is an alias."

"The birth records, high school and college transcripts?" I asked.

"The name Marilyn Todd is in the records, but the records are fakes."

"What did the FBI do about the alert?"

"Nothing. NSA took the lead," Laura said. "Why the hell would the National Security Agency be in Winfield Creek?"

"Beats me, but I'll bet the Bureau knows Todd's real name," I said. "It may get messy around here."

"It's already messy," Laura said. "And we're up to our necks in it. It's bad enough everyone in town believes you killed Todd, and now Monica Love's dead body was found in your bedroom." Laura sighed and rubbed her forehead.

"Not everyone," I said.

"What?" Laura stared, and her sad eyes gave away her conflicted emotions.

"Two people, you and Charley, know I didn't kill Todd or Love. Three people if you count Cree."

"It's the long hours. We are failing, and Mason Dew has dropped off the planet," Laura said.

"OK, let's talk about Monica Love," I said.

"Sam is at your house, and TBI should be there within the hour. The scene of the crime is similar to the Todd case. Too many mixed emotions, Bob. Your bedroom where we—" Laura could not finish her words. I held her arm to comfort her. Her body trembled, and I wished I could hug her, but we were in her office, and that would do her an injustice.

"All the more reason we need each other," I said.

"All I can think about is three women in your life, murdered. The policewoman in me says their murders can't be coincidences."

"Laura, they aren't, and I don't know why they were killed. You know in your heart I didn't do it." She studied me for what seemed like an eternity. Laura's deep penetrating eyes searched my soul.

"You will need a new bed?"

"That and a new bedroom," I said. Relieved she believed me.

"Get a queen size," said Laura.

"I will get a King, a lot more room to roam," I said. "New carpet and paint on the wall. Then the house goes up for sale. Too many ghosts for me to stay there," I said. She gave me a look that melted my heart. "Before Cree hung up he told me something else. He called it a good faith gesture. He said the killer is closer than we think. He said he did not kill Love, and he knows who Love is."

"What's that mean?"

"I don't know," I said. "When the lab results and the autopsy report come back, we may have a clue. I don't know what to believe, if anything, of what Cree said. Maybe we are looking in the wrong places. Let's say, for argument's sake, we accept that Cree did not kill the women. Who does that leave us with?"

"Let's see, we have Dew at the scene of the crime. He could be Todd's killer, but he didn't kill Love," Laura said.

"He didn't strike me to have the gumption to be a cold blooded killer. If we believed Cree, then it is someone close to us. Maybe someone connected to the Lyle family," I said.

"Bob, don't tell me you started to believe in the curse?"

"No, but they could be using the curse mythology or—"

"What?" Laura questioned.

"A serial killer is in our midst."

Laura said, "Todd worked for the NSA, and she had stolen some of their secrets. Seems reasonable to me Todd was assassinated."

"I understand the logic; except Cree is a pro and their kills are neat and tidy. However, it's not unreasonable that he could have made it look like the work of a serial killer," I said. "Let's say that is the how. Then what is the why? And what does he gain?"

Laura laid out a possibility, "Todd had stolen files from the NSA. They sent Cree to retrieve them. The files have to be sensitive at best, maybe top secret. His plan was to get in and out with the hard drive. Something went wrong, and he killed Marilyn."

"Could be, I don't see a reason for Cree to kill Love, though. On the phone, Cree said he and Love had worked together. He trained her, and he said he loved her."

"Cree's playing you, Bob."

"Maybe, but I can't figure out any reason why he would stage an assassination to look like the work of a mad-man, other than to cover his tracks."

Laura said, "We forgot an important part, If Cree killed Todd, why did he have to go back to the house a second time for the hard drive? That blew up my scenario. We have a lot of questions."

"And no answers," I added.

"I'm hungry, want to get some lunch?" I said.

"Sure, let's go to Mary's Place."

"It's a tea room," I said.

"They have finger sandwiches."

"Only women go into the place," I protested.

"Not when you are with me," she said. Then I followed her, wondering how she always managed to get me to do what she wanted.

Chapter 21

"Charley's wife passed away this morning. You going to the funeral Mass?" Laura asked. That didn't sound to me like a question. "No, I'll just pay my respects to Charley. Less than two weeks," I muttered.

"What?"

"When Charley told me about his wife's cancer, he said the end was close."

"I'm going," she said and held her glass up while I refreshed her Champagne.

"I believe they recruited Marilyn at the university," I said. Laura ran her hand across the new Egyptian silk sheets.

"I like the new bed. The sheets are grand, and the Champagne is a nice touch," she changed the subject.

"Glad you approve, figured we had something to celebrate."

"The bedroom do-over is pretty nice. No one would guess a woman was murdered in here," she said.

"I found out that Todd had a Master's degree in cryptology," I said. "That is right up the NSA alley." Laura sat her glass on the nightstand and rolled towards me.

"How did you find that out?"

"I have an FBI connection too."

"We don't need to work the case tonight," she cooed. "We can get our minds off of it for a while and think about us."

"It's time we relieved some stress," I said.

Chapter 22

I poured my usual second cup of coffee, determined to have a few moments of peace and quiet and browse the morning paper. The editorial column, written by Thelma Burke, slammed the Winfield Creek P.D. Burke called me out as the prime suspect still walking about town, and working hand in hand with the Chief of Police. To substantiate her claim, she referenced a Blog, titled Cold Case Thawed, written by an amateur sleuth whose specialty was hounding the police about unsolved murders. *He sounds like another loud mouth that craved attention and cared little about facts and truth.* Thelma had quoted his post that featured the unsolved murders of Thomas Lyle and his sons. From there he connected the notion a copycat killer did Todd and Love. He named me the obvious suspect and called for my arrest. In the next paragraph, he wrote about the small and inexperienced police department. The ringtones from my cell interrupted the small moment of solitude. I thumbed the button and listened, "You and Laura ready to meet?" Cree asked.

"Is that what you called it, a meet? It sounded more like a threat to me."

"Now, Bob, no reason to be hostile."

"I'm tired of your bullshit, Cree, and I'm fed up with unprofessional newspaper editorials, and unethical bloggers," I ranted. Then I breathed in slow and deep to get control of my temper. In a calm tone, I replied to Cree's question. "We agree, tell me where and when."

"I will come to you tonight. Be home. You and I need time to talk first, and Bob, work on the stress. It will kill you before anyone else will." I hung up without speaking another word and decided not to go to the station today. I couldn't allow my stress affect Laura.

I prepped a warm bath and started to develop a defense. Cree could not be trusted, but he knew who killed Marilyn. We had no other choice; we had to work with him. The hot water soothed my tense muscles. I needed a good plan. A stone cold killer was coming to visit.

I snapped on the pen light, looked at my watch, twenty-two fifty hours. My left hand gripped the 45, and with extra ammo pouches I was ready to handle anything Cree dished out. The cell chimed, "Hello."

"Don't say a word," said Cree. "Pretend it's a wrong number and listen to me. Your house is under surveillance. I will be in touch. Just say out loud, you have the wrong number, and then hang up."

Chapter 23

Who, other than Cree, would put surveillance on my house? My anger boiled. The backlit cell phone screen hampered my night vision. It took twenty minutes for my eyes to readjust to the dark. I moved from room to room, and I watched for any sign of movement outside.

I retrieved my portable bug detector from the closet to scan for radio/cell phone frequencies. That device could detect telephone taps, bugs, and even spy-cams. I used it many times when on active duty when traveling abroad. This was its first use in retirement. I scanned the house, and did not find any detectable bugs. Then I exited through the front door, pretending to go for a walk.

I had slipped on my dark green jacket to cover the forty-five and baggy trousers to cover my black nylon suit. I carried a small pack that contained ammo, water, a compass, a flashlight equipped with an infrared filter, and a pair of night vision goggles.

I strolled down the porch steps and scanned for signs of hard targets watching the house. The tree line was about seventy-five feet from the front and to the left side of my house. The right side was adjacent to the driveway, and the road dead-ended on my drive. The back had five feet of clearance.

Concealed surveillance was possible from several directions. To set up surveillance at the rear of the house or on the left side required a five-mile trek from Pine Creek road across the mountain. Then they would have to travel down a steep slope to get in position. My gut told me they would take the easier route and set up to the front. That gave them access to a vehicle for a fast exit.

Cree had warned me, He must have been close. The forty-five was positioned where my left hand could draw the weapon. A quick draw with the left hand was an effective surprise since most people assume a right-handed draw. Thoughts circled my mind. *How many people are involved? Where is Cree?*

The odds were better with him on my side. Cree didn't provide any actionable Intel. Therefore, I had to prepare for the unexpected. I walked near the Explorer palming the bug detector. Clean. I laid the bug detector on the rear bumper and walked down the road, stopping every so often. I pretended to tie my shoelace or gaze at the stars while checking my six for a tail. It was easy enough to check the left and right sides close to the road, but I would have to go into the woods to find the culprits.

I walked about one klick, to a dirt access road used by firefighters to move equipment used to fight forest fires. Fresh tire tracks indicated that a vehicle had recently driven on the path. Nonetheless, the dirt road was also a favorite place for teens to park. After another half klick, I left the road and entered the woods. Then I crouched down to wait.

Satisfied no one was following, I stripped off the green jacket and outer clothing. If Cree made a try for me at the house, I had a surprise waiting for him. However, I didn't think he had concocted the surveillance story. I pulled the stocking cap down over my face and started through the woods back towards the access road.

The body suit was a Kevlar woven fabric that provided a feeling of invincibility. A false sense of security, but at least it could prevent a mortal wound. The suit rendered my figure close to invisible in the night woods. Using stealth skills, I snaked in and around the trees, moved back up the slope. Not knowing where Cree was hiding concerned me. A vehicle sat on the dirt access road, fifty yards ahead. Getting closer, I saw it was a black SUV.

This was not a couple of teens out for a night of necking. I gave the vehicle a wide berth, moving at an angle, and then turned to walk within twenty paces from the back of the SUV. I squatted at the center of the rear bumper. It had no license plate and no tailpipe, showing it to be an electric motor vehicle. The deep-tinted rear windows made it impossible to see inside.

I moved left and peered around the vehicle. The driver had the window down to release cigarette smoke. Two voices were audible. I inched along the vehicle and stopped in the blind spot. The reflection of the man's profile in the mirror was like a shadow. I was not able to see his features.

"The house is quiet," the man in the driver's seat, said.

"Relax, he's asleep," a woman's voice said. "He doesn't have a clue we're on to him."

"They check in yet?" The man asked.

"No, in fifteen minutes," she said.

I backed up to the rear bumper and picked my way a short distance up the hill where I could see the vehicle roof. A small communications dish stuck out through the open sunroof pointed in the direction of my house. Cree had not lied about the surveillance. A million questions raced through my mind. *Are they government? Why are they targeting my house? How long have they been listening?*

A black SUV did not always point to a government agency, but it was a good assumption for starters. The NSA topped my list of suspects. They were going through me to get to Cree.

I moved up the slope and stopped where I could see the faint outline of my house through the trees. A swishing sound and rustled brush startled me. Through the night-vision goggles, I saw an owl with his claws clamped on a small rodent. The owl surprised someone else. I focused on the spot where a figure made a slight movement. A shooter was lying on the ground beside a patch of briar. I crept closer. Controlled my breathing, I stayed close to the tree trunks with the forty-five in my hand. I slipped within a comfortable distance behind the man. A sniper waiting for his target; he didn't have a spotter.

About fifteen yards to the right of him were two more figures, inside the tree line with weapons aimed at my front door. They had to be here for Cree. Otherwise, they would have gunned me down when I stepped outside. They knew Cree would be here tonight. A hand grasped my arm. Startled and defensive, I brought the forty-five around.

"Stop, before they hear us," the familiar voice whispered.

"What the hell?" My heart thumped, I almost spat my words.

"You're focused on what's in front of you and forgot about your six. They knew about our meeting," Jack said.

"NSA," I said.

"No, they're private," he said.

"How tough are they?"

"Not tough enough. What did you bring?"

"Forty-five Commander, and two knives," I said.

"We'll take them out," Cree said.

"I only kill in self-defense."

"That's easy for you to say. They're after me," Cree stated in a low sharp tone. Then he crawled away.

Chapter 24

I employed skills used in Nam and quietly angled to his left flank and closed in on the shooter. He was in a prone position with a sniper rifle pointed toward the house. His focus was straight ahead. He didn't hear me. I counted to five. Then between heartbeats, I threw my full body weight on his back and ran my left arm under his chin and around his neck. With my right arm, I covered his mouth and nose. His hands came up and grabbed my arm. He tried to roll. He could not breathe or yell, and in a few seconds, he blacked out. With his strength gone, his body went limp. I pulled his belt off, brought both arms behind his back, and buckled them together. In one fluid motion, I snagged the rifle, an M100 with a scope. I folded the bipod and crawled towards the next target, anticipating that Jack had neutralized any shooters in his area.

The cloud-covered moon gave us an advantage. Just a few inches from the next shooter, I encountered a brush pile. It would have taken too much time to go around, and I could not cross it without making noise. Then I tried an old movie trick.

"Hey buddy," I said to the man.

"Be quiet," the man replied. The man was on his stomach and turned his head towards me. The brush pile provided cover. I whispered again. Agitated and swearing the man rose to his knees. A stream of moonlight slipped between clouds and splashed through the tree canopy. The target realized I was not his partner.

Without hesitation, and before the man could bring his weapon to bear, I sprung over the brush and jammed the butt of the M110 in his face. He yelled as bone and cartilage popped. The man instinctively squeezed the trigger on his Uzi that sent bullets through the air, missing me, but alarming the others.

I stayed close to the ground and squirmed through brush and between trees in a crosswise direction from the other gunmen. They didn't know my exact location so they fanned the air with lead, amateurs. Muzzle fire lit up the woods, and tree bark sailed through the air like rocks skipping across a pond. The racket from the Uzis echoed down the mountain for several seconds.

When they went quiet, I looked up. Settled in, I unfolded the legs on the M110 and through the scope I saw the third shooter inserting a fresh clip. He had not moved from his original position. I panned the rifle and spotted another shooter moving to join him. I moved again to put distance between us. I wondered what happened to Cree. My foot snagged a root, and I fell to the ground. The racket from brush and broken twigs gave away my position.

I hugged the ground swearing when rounds from automatic weapons spit through the humid air. "Damn, how many gunmen are out here?" I mumbled.

I looked through the scope, and three more black-clad bodies were running towards my position, trying to overrun me. I squirmed to the right about three yards, setup up the rifle and then took down one of the three charging mercenaries with a shot to his leg. The other two dove to the ground, and I moved before they could relocate my position. Bullets threw up dirt and bark in the general area where I had been.

I retreated fifty yards and turned up the slope. "Damn I'm rusty," I swear under my breath. They weren't sure where I was, and panic began to settle in. They fired weapons in all directions. They were definitely not former special forces. With that approach, they were more likely to hit each other accidentally than to get me. A little luck was on my side.

I found a small area of limestone. I set the tripod on the rock and aimed at two combatants squatted down together. I steadied my finger and started to apply pressure when the sound of a siren wailed. The two men darted in the direction of the parked SUV. I pulled the rifle down from the rock, rolled on my back, and breathed in the smell of battle. My upper right arm burned and throbbed. Memories of another place halfway around the world flashed before my eyes. Sweat rolled down my face like rain. I ripped off the headgear, breathed deep. It had been a long time since my last firefight. I told myself, "You held your own and survived for another battle, old man."

I walked the area and retrieved the man I shackled with his belt. Jack Cree was nowhere in sight. He had left me. The SUV was gone. The flashing lights of police cars raced up the road, streaking through the woods. I grabbed my prisoner who was semi-conscious and walked towards the house.

Chapter 25

In the time, it had taken me to exit the woods, Winfield Creek's finest, the Sheriff Department, and Tennessee Highway Patrol had the road blocked. Flashing lights bounced off the house.

"Halt, Police!" A voice blasted over a bullhorn. Spotlights blinded me, and I dropped the M110 at my side, threw one hand in the air, and held on to my prisoner with my left. The outlines of several officers in helmets and vests trotted towards me with weapons at the ready. The officers stopped, and then from behind them I heard the familiar voice, "Here we go again."

"Detective Reynolds, it could not have been anyone else. You work 24/7?"

"You're in deep crap here, Agent Bob, and you still give me lip. At least you dropped your weapon," Reynolds said.

"It was Special Agent and soon going to be Private Investigator. Didn't want to give you a reason to shoot me, Detective. This man and several others tried to kill me. Look in the woods and you will find another one with a leg wound. I've been busy, defending myself."

Sam used his flashlight to motion a patrol officer towards the woods. He passed the man I captured to a sheriff deputy, and then Sam pushed my face to the ground, and jammed his knee hard in my back. He locked the handcuffs tight, sending a clear message of his dislike for me. He grabbed my cuffed hands and yanked me to my feet.

"Sam, we got a wounded man over here," an Officer yelled. Reynolds groaned, and I got a glimpse of Laura's cruiser when she pulled up behind the fleet. She walked fast towards Sam, "What have we got here, Sam? Why is Snow cuffed?" Her voice was terse. I could feel her angry eyes on me.

Reynolds said, "On a stake-out at the Bean Pot for a crack dealer when dispatch radioed a report of automatic weapons fire in this area." Sam's large hand gripped my arm, and he pulled me towards his cruiser. I was a rag doll in the grip of an overgrown child. Laura followed.

"Special Agent, Bob." Sam's words dripped with a mixture of glee and hate. "He came out of the woods with that rifle." He pointed to the M110 sniper rifle now in the possession of Officer O'Connor. "We got the man Snow pulled out of the woods, there's another one who had been knocked unconscious and a third one had a gunshot wound." Laura listened. Then she walked over to the officers in the woods without saying a word to me.

"Pull your cruisers down into the yard, and shine the head lights in the woods," Laura shouted.

"Anyone see a black SUV when you drove up the road?" I asked. Reynolds shifted his weight with the usual disdain.

"No sir," a Tennessee Highway Patrol officer said.

"Just my luck," I said.

Sam released the Tennessee Highway Patrol and the County Sheriff's Deputies. "We have this punk under control." Reynolds threw me in the back seat and pulled his unmarked down the yard towards the woods where Laura stood.

"Sam, call an ambulance. Make sure everyone is gloved up and retrieve any weapons and spent cartridges, and tape off the area."

Reynolds left to carry out the orders, and then Laura turned in my direction. She opened the cruiser door and leaned in,

"Alright," she exhaled a sigh. "Explain this, Robert!" I told her about Cree's call. She looked unhappy that I had agreed to meet with him alone. By the time the ambulance arrived to take care of the wounded, the officers on the scene had one weapon and a bag full of shell casings. Laura called an EMT over to dress my flesh wound when Reynolds called out. I turned to see his smile. "Smiling at me? That is a first, Detective."

"Don't get used to it. You're a magnet for trouble. I'm almost afraid to stand next to you. You captured one man, busted another one's nose, and shot a third guy in the leg. We've recovered an Uzi, a scoped sniper rifle, and enough spent shells for a small army. You're dressed in black with infrared headgear, a forty-five, and two knives. Looked to me you were on the hunt. You were carrying the rifle when I saw you."

"How do you explain why those gunmen were here?" I asked.

"I can't, yet. Since my boss gives you the benefit of the doubt, I have to walk a thin line to stay out of her doghouse." He turned me around and unlocked the cuffs.

"If I were on the hunt, there wouldn't be a prisoner or wounded. The others would not have escaped," I said.

"You think you're a real badass."

"No, I'm not a badass, just trained better. The sniper rifle belonged to the man I pulled out of the woods. I wrestled it from him."

Reynolds said, "I suppose you're trying to convince me someone sent out a sniper with a small army to take you down?"

"I don't know, but they were here with extreme malice."

"Too bad they didn't succeed," Reynolds sniped.

"By the way, how bad is Bright's dog house?"

"You'll know when she figures out I was right about you." He walked away chuckling and shaking his head. "We should lock you up and throw away the key, agent man!"

"What's that all about?" Laura said walking over. I shrugged it off. "We've done all we can tonight. We'll go back over the ground in daylight."

"Want some coffee?"

"Yes," she replied, "and you're going to explain to me what happened out here, and why you didn't call me for help. You let me walk into this mess blind."

"You're mad."

"Yes, I'm angry. We're working together on this case and you are grandstanding. You make me look like a smitten woman in front of my detective."

Chapter 26

Briefing Laura on the incident took an hour. Then we spent another hour making up before falling asleep around 3:00 AM. We woke at six and showered. Laura fussed over my minor gunshot wound. Afterward, we decided to eat breakfast at the Grinder before going to the office. Laura pulled away, and I followed in the Explorer.

My cell rang. "Hey, have to take a rain check on breakfast, duty calls," Laura said.

"Too bad. Anything I should know about?"

"Nope. Mayor Pickle called me in to have a talk," Laura said.

"About?"

"My guess is she wants to talk about the incident last night and the Todd case then about us."

"That going to be a problem?" I inquired.

"I got it. Enjoy your breakfast and stay out of trouble. Don't go near the woods either. Let the forensic techs work the scene. By the end of the day, if we're lucky, we will have more evidence."

"I doubt they're going to find anything other than more cartridges."

"Nevertheless, we have one in lock up and two in the hospital. The one guy's leg is in bad shape, and he lost a lot of blood. The other just has a broken nose."

"A 7.62 round does some damage."

"Mind what I said. Stay out of trouble."

"It's breakfast, Laura. How much trouble can I get into?"

"You're like a lightning rod for trouble."

"Reynolds had similar words for me. I might develop a complex," I said.

"Yeah right," Laura said and then hung up.

At the Grinder, the waitress delivered the eggs and bacon with a pleasant smile. I salted and peppered the eggs and was prepared to dig in when a man dressed in shorts and a t-shirt approached the table. He looked like a chubby, forty-something tourist. He asked to join me. There were plenty of empty seats, but out of curiosity, I agreed.

"Bob Snow," I reached my hand across the table.

"We have a mutual friend," the man said without shaking my hand. He didn't give his name.

"Who might that be?" I asked.

"Our friend told me you have a need for a plumber."

"Don't have any broken pipes," I replied.

"Our friend said you have a plugged drain. It needs a special tool to fix it, and he said your equipment is broken." The man sat back in the chair. The waitress approached to take his order, and he waved her off.

"His last name is Cree," I said.

"If you say so," the man said. "The company truck will be at your place this afternoon. Be home, the plumber's name is Frankie."

"You look like a tourist, not like a man who carried Cree's bags. I want to know why he had ducked out on me last night and where he is now." Without another word, the man stood and left the building. I finished my breakfast, confused about what just happened. Laura's warning to stay out of trouble blared in my mind.

Chapter 27

A gray van, with *Elmer's Plumbing,* stenciled on the door in bright orange letters, rolled into my driveway at noon. A long-legged chestnut-haired woman wearing skintight coveralls strolled to the rear of the van. She wore a ball cap with the 'Power T' emblem. She pulled open the door and retrieved a toolbox. I stared out the window and wondered what kind of plumber Cree lined up.

"You need your pipes cleaned?" Her tone was like silk. I strained to pull my eyes away from her cleavage.

"So I've been told." I stepped back and opened the door wider. She entered. I noted the way she brushed past me and placed her toolbox on the counter. *How will I explain this to Laura?* I killed that thought then said, "Your name is Elmer?"

"No, he's my brother. He drums up the business, and I fix the pipes," she teased with an emphasis on the double meaning.

"Don't worry Mr. Snow. I'm good at what I do. You won't be disappointed." She removed an instrument from the toolbox. I recognized the bug detector right away.

"I have the first gen model," I said.

"That's why it didn't work," she said.

"How do you know it didn't work?"

"Because I'm here, fella." She made a few adjustments and then walked through the living room. I sat in the recliner and pretended to read.

"Make yourself comfortable, Mr. Snow. This won't take long," she said. After about fifteen minutes, she had scanned all the rooms. She returned and held out her palm to reveal four small electronic listening devices.

"Your pipes are cleared now, Mr. Snow."

"Great, thanks. How much do I owe you?"

"My fee has been paid, in advance," she smiled, picked up her toolbox, and glided out the door. I watched until she drove away. In the pit of my stomach, I felt a small twinge of relief conflicted with regret. After the van had rolled out of sight, I went to the closet and retrieved my bug detector. The device found four active bugs. One in each bedroom, the hall, and she had planted one in the living room.

Right under my nose. She was good. I deduced that it had to be Cree who hired this outfit to bug my place. I wondered who had planted the other bugs, the ones she had handed me. It was possible those bugs were decoys to make me believe they had been there. That made sense, but Cree had to know I would find his devices. I wondered what he would gain from this escapade. It didn't matter. I now had a way to feed him bogus information.

Chapter 28

I stored the bug detector in the closet and headed out to the police station, eager to ask Laura about her meeting with the Mayor. I also wanted to fill her in on this new development. When I rolled into the parking lot, Laura was leaving her office by way of the rear door. She waved. I pulled into a stall next to her unmarked car. Laura opened the passenger door and started to drill me. "Who's the woman?"

"How did you know?"

"Small town. You need variety?"

"It's not like that. You knew she had been there. Then you also know she didn't stay that long."

"Long enough for you," Laura snarled then paused. Her eyes narrowed, and a slow grin changed the scowl across her face.

"You were jerking my chain again," I sighed.

"Lighten up, Robert. I had to put some humor in our relationship."

"Is that what we have, a relationship?"

"Don't let the word frighten you," Laura said. "I didn't use the L-word."

"The meeting with the Mayor, how did it go?" I changed the subject, struggling not to let my aggravation show.

"Still have my job, for now," Laura said and strolled back to her office door. "Mayor Pickle told me to close the Todd case, regardless of the fact Monica Love had not been formally identified as the suspect. She fit the description. That was good enough."

"Convenient. She's dead and cannot defend herself," I replied. "Did the Mayor mention anything about us?"

"Plenty, but the Mayor doesn't run my private life." Laura stopped and looked me in the eye, "She's satisfied this case can be closed, 'since we have the dead psycho-killer in the morgue', and those were her words."

"Love may or may not have killed Marilyn. If not, then the killer is still out there and will get away. Cree's warning still nags at me. 'The killer is closer than you think.'"

"I feel it too," she said. Laura's demeanor was all business when we walked into her office.

"We still haven't found out why Marilyn came to Winfield Creek," I said.

"I know, but we close the murder investigation, make the Mayor happy, and get the town folks off our backs. We don't stop going after Cree. We dig deeper into Todd's activities. If we have a nasty killer on the loose, he or she will let their guard down," she said.

"We do that, and we cave-in to the political pressure. If it does turn out Love is not the killer, we will have ruined her reputation. I don't like taking the easy way out, Laura."

"No, I don't either," Laura said.

"The lady plumber planted bugs in the house," I said. "Nothing happened between us."

"That's interesting."

"Which part?" I said.

"Both, and the fact that you would even think you had a chance with her," she laughed with a nervous twitch in her voice.

"While you were meeting with Mayor Pickle, a man approached me. He looked like a tourist; he said we have a mutual friend. The mutual friend told this man I needed a plumber. My equipment was broken, and I couldn't fix the problem, the man said to me."

"Elmer's plumbing," Laura said.

"Right. The plumber showed me some devices she claimed to find planted in the house. When she left, I used my equipment and found the bugs she planted."

"Did you remove them?"

"No, not until I'm sure of what Cree is up to."

"The man said Cree?"

"He didn't verbalize it. His body language confirmed it."

"What if you're wrong and it's not Cree? What would Cree gain by bugging your house?" Laura asked.

"If it's not him, then we're in more trouble than we bargained for. Could be FBI, NSA, or some rogue outfit. In any case, removing the bugs will tip them off. Leaving the bugs in place can work to our advantage."

Laura was silent, and then she said, "Alright, are there cameras?" I shook my head.

"Good, then we won't be giving someone a peep show."

"So you believe me that nothing happened between the plumber and me?"

"Don't know why, but I do believe you. I checked out Elmer's Plumbing, and they have an office in Johnston City. They don't have an employee that matched the woman's description."

Sam Reynolds interrupted our conversation when he barged into the office. "Chief, the Park Rangers found Mason Dew, dead. His body was under thick brush at the base of a steep slope, a bullet hole in his head."

Chapter 29

"This case is getting stranger by the day. Todd pretended to be someone she wasn't. She had worked in a dangerous field with cruel people, and I still haven't ruled out that Cree killed Todd and Monica Love or why he would have killed them. Cree is playing games. The way those women were killed is not consistent with a professional hit. Then there is Mason Dew, the sole witness that placed Monica at the crime scene, shot in the head and rolled down the side of the mountain."

"I see what you mean, Robert. You are getting obsessed with this case. A thing like this investigation can bring a man down," Charley said.

"I can't leave it alone, Charley. I apologize. The last thing you need is to listen to me vent. Especially, right after you lost Elizabeth."

"It's painful, yes, even when it was expected; one is not prepared to accept the end when it comes. The worst part is the empty house. Most of my time was devoted to taking care of Elizabeth. Now I have nothing to do, but dwelling on me is selfish. The loneliness makes me want David to come back home. No matter how all of this turns out, I can't thank you enough for what you did for David."

"It's what friends do," I said.

"I don't like to see anyone lose their life, even a criminal, but I'm glad Monica is out of David's life," Charley said. "I'm confident the police and you will fit the pieces together and solve these murders."

"If the publicity doesn't get me killed first," I said. "Someone is feeding the press."

"Feeding them? You have given them plenty of fodder to chew on. And forgive me for being blunt; in the process you have soiled Chief Bright's reputation."

"I hear you Charley, but Laura is a woman who knows what she wants. Steaks are done." I placed the T-bones on the plates with baked potatoes and green beans, "Laura can take care of herself. She's her own woman. No one, including me, makes Laura Bright do anything she doesn't want to do."

"I've known Laura a long time. She has always been strong-willed," Charley said. "I do appreciate the invite to dinner. Laura was right about one thing."

"Only one thing," I said.

"Well, for sure more than one, but she bragged about your cooking." Charley said the blessing and we enjoyed our dinner in silence.

After dinner Charley and I stood on the front porch sipping hot cups of herbal tea. "Charley, you were right when you said I am obsessed with this case, and it's not because most of the people around here think I killed those women. It goes back to Nam. A good friend of mine was found dead, and his death was ruled a suicide. I knew better, but I couldn't prove it. It's why I got into CID, to learn the profession and find out who killed him and why."

"How did you know he didn't commit suicide, Robert?"

"I just knew. We had been friends a long time, and it was not in his nature to kill himself."

"War can change a man," Charley said. "I ministered to a man who took his own life, and I did not see that in him. People can hide a barrel of problems deep inside themselves. His wife didn't see the signs either."

"I know what I know. Can't explain it. I buried myself in work and solved many cases. I could never get close to proving the truth and along the way, I lost another friend. A woman I knew died, in my house at Meade. It was ruled a break-in, and she got in the way. I worked the case hard, but never could find any evidence to prove she had been the target." The herbal tea was soothing. Charley was easy to talk to, and my inhibition against confession was weak.

"Well then," said Charley, "After a stellar career, other than the two cases you mentioned, you retired to Winfield Creek, took a lover and she was murdered the morning after your first date. I see your problem, Robert. I've been romantically close to one woman who died, my wife. You've been close to two who've died in gruesome ways."

"Todd had been a dinner date, nothing more."

"How many attempts have been made on your life, Robert?"

"War doesn't count. Including the most recent, I'd say a half dozen or more."

"You need to get right with God," said Charley.

"You broke your record, Charley." He looked puzzled.

"You have been in my house several hours before you gave me the sermon."

"I know you're annoyed, but it's called evangelizing."

"I'm not annoyed, Charley. You're a good friend and a cleric. It was expected. Will God protect me from my enemies?"

"Of course he can. However, if your enemies succeed, have you thought about hell?"

"Yeah, my enemies can go to hell," I said.

"You know that's not what I meant."

"If God does exist, why would he be concerned with me? I've never given Him much thought."

"Love, God is love. Hate is the food of His enemies. Think about a conversion, surrender the hate you're savoring within yourself, Robert."

"Anger and hate fuel my desire to find those killers."

"What makes you think it's more than one?" Before I answered, Charley said, "Laura's right. You can cook." I was glad he changed the subject.

It was much later when Charley got into his Rover and drove away. The night air was warm and thick with humidity. The woods were loud with cicada song.

David had broken Charley's heart when he shacked up with Monica Love. Charley lost his wife to cancer and estranged from his son. Somehow, Charley had kept it together. He was a tough man.

Chapter 30

I didn't have time to cool down from my run before the cell chimed. Laura's number showed on the caller ID. "Good morning," I answered.

"You sound chipper. Have a nice dinner with Charley?"

"We did. He's somewhat lost. I think I helped him," I said. "On the other hand, he accused me of sullying your reputation."

She laughed it off, "It'll take Charley some time; he is well grounded in his faith. I'm not worried about him. Bob, the reason I called is we received Monica's autopsy report. The pathologist discovered she had artificial caps on her teeth. He pried them off and x-rayed her real teeth. Monica Love is Elaine Keefe."

"Not surprised she had an alias. I remember Cree alluded that we didn't know her. Nothing with this case is as it should be," I said.

"Elaine Keefe! Elaine freaking Keefe! Does that name ring a bell?" Laura said.

"Should it?" I asked.

"Elaine Keefe, a top fiction writer in the nineties. She disappeared without a trace in two thousand and one. Many surmised she had been killed."

"She has been, now," I said.

"Good observation, Captain Obvious. The question is why did Keefe do a disappearing act? She went to great lengths to change her identity, not just her teeth. She also had some plastic surgery around her eyes, her fingerprints altered, and added tattoos. My friend at the FBI said she had an arrest record on February of 2001. He wouldn't say why. They didn't charge her, but she remained a person of interest. The plots she created in her books involved mercenaries for hire, government sanctioned assassinations, and black ops programs. All of her books were best sellers. The last book she published, <u>The Badge of Deceit</u>, four months before her arrest, stayed on the New York Times best seller list sixteen weeks."

"We need to get a copy of that book," I said. "Plus, can you have Sam dig up old newspaper clippings, videos, anything he can find on her?"

"Already on it. Listen to this - her estimated net worth at the time of her disappearance was twenty-five million," said Laura. I cradled the phone between my cheek and shoulder and fumbled with my iPad. A quick search on Elaine Keefe returned several photos with links to news stories and blogs.

"An attractive woman, nothing like Monica Love," I said.

"The plastic surgeon did a good job."

"I'm reading a blogger's piece that stated Keefe always maintained her books were works of fiction. However, the blogger went on to say that much of what she wrote struck a chord of truth, so much so, that many of her readers and some bigwigs on Capitol Hill believed she had an informant inside the federal government. The blogger claimed the FBI arrested her with the intent to discover the identity of her source. He then writes that it's his belief the government killed her and disposed of her body, Hoffa style."

"That was interesting," Laura said.

"Why did you call your FBI friend?"

"He called me, about Mason Dew's body, discovered inside the Park, federal property. FBI has the investigation, and they suspect Dew was shot on the trail. His body pushed over the edge of the mountain."

"The FBI has the lead in our case. Is your friend, what did you say his name is, the investigating Agent?" I said.

"I didn't say, and no he's not the lead. A Special Agent from D.C. will be taking over the investigation. Some bigwig in the bureau. Are you coming in today?"

"No—how about dinner?"

"Your place or mine?" she said.

"Let's do yours. We can order in pizza."

"Sounds good to me, and I will cook breakfast in the morning," she said.

"I'll go for that."

"Michael Durant is his name," Laura said.

"The bigwig from D.C.?"

"No, my friend. He has never been anything except a friend."

I decided to change the subject. "Cree claims he didn't kill Marilyn or Monica. It's still hard for me to believe him. I think he knew Monica was Elaine Keefe. She worked with him. She might have outlived her usefulness, and he decided to make it look like the same killer did both women."

"I see where you're going; two brutal murders by one person who is not a pro. Dew was killed pro style. If Cree killed Dew and not the women, that would mean we still have another killer in town," she said.

"Yes it does. It's even possible, as unlikely as it sounds, that Cree hasn't killed anyone. That could mean one killer did all three," I said.

"Using a different MO on Dew," Laura added.

"It's another angle. I would give anything to get my hands on that hard drive Cree took from Marilyn's house," I said.

"Did Cree call to set up the meeting?"

"Not yet. Strange because he made it sound like time was of the essence."

"I'll bring a copy of 'Badge of Deceit.' We can do some homework," Laura said. "I'd like to go back over the crime scene reports too. We're missing something." I agreed and hung up anticipating a wonderful evening ahead.

Chapter 31

In an instant, I sighted the intruder's head. "Reynolds, why the devil are you breaking into my house?" I lowered the weapon.

"Your back door was unlocked, Snow. I need your help."

Dumbfounded, I said, "You couldn't knock? Why do you need my help? It's not like we're buddies?"

"I didn't want anyone to see me come here alone."

"That was difficult to accomplish. Everyone in town knows my business. You might as well come on in the living room and have a seat," I said. I laid the gun on the bar and fetched Reynolds a bottle of cold water. His shirt and waistband were soaked with sweat. "Not even noon and the heat and humidity are at the top of the scale. You must have walked a long way."

"I came down the back trail," Reynolds huffed, short of breath. "Has Chief Bright told you about Darrell? He used to be on the force?"

"The cop that got himself involved with dealing crystal meth?"

"Yes, a friend of mine. It hit me hard. Anyway, I suspected he had not worked alone. I have been looking into the possibility Darrell's drug business included another cop on the force."

"You need something else to drink, Sam?"

"The water will be okay," he said and drained the bottle. I gave him another one. He took a gulp and said, "Mason Dew, he wasn't who you think—"

"A lot of that going around; you have any ideas who killed Dew?" I said.

"Yes, O'Connor," he said and took a long pull on the water bottle. He handed me the empty plastic and indicated he would like another one.

"Officer O'Connor?" I was surprised because O'Connor appeared to an honest cop. "What made you think he shot Dew?"

"He owns a 22 caliber handgun."

"A lot of people do, Sam. What would have been O'Connor's motive?"

"Greed. He collaborated with Darrell. They operated a meth lab, and it was a lucrative business. O'Connor and Darrell were inseparable on and off the job."

"The way I heard it, O'Connor was the one who discovered Darrell's enterprise and reported him," I said.

"Yes, but O'Connor didn't find Darrell's lab. He already knew about it. Darrell was the chemist and O'Connor managed the sales. They had a large enterprise, and I believed Mason Dew had been one of their runners."

"O'Connor double-crossed his friend and partner?"

"That's what I'm saying."

"Why? Without the chemist, O'Connor is out of the product." Sam shrugged, "Why did you bring this to me and not your boss?" I asked.

"Chief Bright is good. She knows her business, but O'Connor is like a favorite son to her."

"You don't think Chief Bright will believe you. You are her detective. You get the benefit of the doubt."

"She doesn't like me."

That didn't surprise me, "You have proof to back up your statement?"

"Yes," Reynolds said.

"Let's say I believed you. I still don't like you not going to Chief Bright. Show me your proof."

"I went up the mountain with the FBI to where Dew's body had been recovered on federal property. Darrell's cabin was three miles in the other direction outside the park boundary. On a hunch, I went to the cabin."

"Wait, you left the FBI investigation to trek through the woods in another direction?"

"I made an excuse to leave. They didn't need me hanging around. So I went back down the trail and drove my unmarked to another road. It intersected with the trail that leads to the cabin. Dew's daypack and sleeping bag were still in the cabin. Food wrappers and cans were laying everywhere. Dew had lived there, and I found packs of crystal meth." Sam paused to drain the bottled water. "There were signs of a struggle. I know that cabin is where he killed Dew."

"Who?"

"O'Connor," he said.

"You have proof O'Connor killed him?"

"Just my instincts," Reynolds said.

"Then don't mention O'Connor," I said, "The evidence to

implicate the killer, whoever that was, may be in the cabin." My thoughts swirled. This was a bombshell, and red flags were popping up. Reynolds hated my guts, and he definitely did not trust me. I couldn't figure out why he dumped this in my lap.

"Where's the cabin located?"

"It's off a dirt road in the hills near Newport. The abandoned cabin sits back into the woods," Sam said.

"Can you write out some directions?" I said, getting a tablet and a pen from the secretary.

"Sure I can. Don't advise you go up there alone."

"Why?"

"Could stumble upon a pot farm and get shot or trip a bobby trap," Sam smiled. I wondered if he was egging me on.

"The fellow you mentioned before—"

"Cree," I said.

"Yeah, think he's involved with Dew's death too?"

"Don't know," I said.

"The dead woman in your bed. You reckon this Cree guy killed her?"

"He said he didn't, but Cree is a hired gun. I'm sure Chief Bright's better suited to discuss the case with you." I knew Laura held back information from Sam, but she was the one to whom he needed to talk.

"Like I said, Bob. You don't mind if I call you Bob?"

"That's fine." I said, "You getting chummy with me?"

"Not quite. I know you two are close, but Chief Bright doesn't trust me or like me. She did not promote me to Detective. If she had her way, I would not be on the force. My mother is an influential woman who is close friends with Mayor Pickle. Mom was a substantial contributor to the Mayor's political ambitions."

"I get the picture. Mayor Pickle promoted you," I said.

"She ordered Chief Bright to move me up to Detective," said Sam.

"Politics is a rough business, where money flows like a river. Nevertheless, you have to tell this story to Chief Bright."

Chapter 32

Reynolds left the house in the same direction he entered. I gave him two bottles of water and warned him that a big man dehydrated faster. Sam's visit left me with even more questions. He implicated Officer O'Connor in a criminal enterprise with Darrell. He connected Mason Dew to their crime, and he said O'Connor had killed Dew. Reynolds did not know about the listening devices in the house. Cree knew what I knew.

I walked outside, pulled my cell out, and dialed Jon Pate. Laura didn't know I had an acquaintance in the bureau also. Jon Pate worked at the Hoover building, and on several occasions, when I was still in CID, I passed him solid leads on several serial killers. On the third ring, he answered, "Jon Pate."

"Hello, Jon. Bob Snow."

"How's retirement, Bob? I can't wait to join you in the social security ranks."

"You'll never leave the bureau," I said.

"For what it's worth, I think you got a raw deal at Meade," He said.

"Thanks, I appreciate the words. This is not a social call, Jon."

"What can I do you for?"

"Hear about the murder in Winfield Creek, Tennessee?"

"Sure, and I know you're a suspect."

"Was, and now I'm helping the Chief of Police, Laura Bright with the investigation. Our witness, Mason Dew, was murdered in the National Park."

"That will be handled by the Knoxville office, under my supervision."

"So you're the big wig from D.C."

Jon laughed. "A flunky is more like it. Dew was killed on Federal property. Marilyn Todd was linked to a federal agency. My boss asked me to come down and lend my assistance."

I called to ask you to check out two names for me: Jack Cree and Elaine Keefe. I need to know what the connection is between them."

"Elaine Keefe, that name is a hot topic. Everyone in the Bureau and every other government agency is familiar with her. Jack Cree doesn't ring a bell, but I'll check the name and get back to you."

"I have a voice recording of Cree and a picture of a woman's body whose dental imprints identified her as Elaine Keefe. I'll email them to you."

"Good, I'll need all the information I can get. When I come down there, I need to hit the ground running."

"One more item, Jon. I got a tip on an abandoned cabin just off the Federal property. The informant says Mason Dew had lived there. Maybe nothing, but I'm going to check it out."

"That cabin could contain evidence central to the investigation. Special Agent Michael Durant works out of the Knoxville office. You can call him."

"Thanks, Jon," I said.

"Don't worry my friend. I will collect. By the way, I miss the leads. We had put away quite a few bad guys, thanks to you."

"I plan to do some private cop work. Might scare up some business for you, Jon." We ended the call. I had every intention to share the information on the cabin with Michael Durant, but not until I had a chance to check it out first.

Chapter 33

The drive over the mountain above Newport had some of the most crooked roads I had ever driven. I planned to examine the cabin and then drive back to Laura's house in time for pizza. I pulled off the blacktop onto the dirt road indicated on Reynolds' hand-drawn map. Sam's scribble was hard to read. I held the map between my thumb and index finger with both hands gripped on the steering wheel.

After five miles of dust, bumps, and tires dropping into washed out ruts, I stopped close to the large boulder that had the splash of black paint, as indicated on the map. It marked the entry point of the trail that led to the cabin.

I locked the Explorer, grabbed my daypack filled with water, protein snacks, and extra clips for my handgun. According to Reynolds notations, the trail climbed up the slope towards the ridge and then ran parallel to the ridge for about a half mile.

Thirteen hundred hours, I set the timer on my watch to monitor my pace. *It should be easy to find the cabin,* I thought. Once there, I'd look for evidence to substantiate Sam's story that Dew had been staying at the cabin, and determine if any clues confirmed a Meth trade.

I had no real reason to believe Reynolds had me out on a wild goose chase, but his sudden decision to confide in me felt strange. Nevertheless, I had to check out Reynolds story. If he was playing games, then I planned to confront him the next day.

After a hundred yards of fighting overhanging limbs and thick brush, I stopped for a sip of water. The humidity was thick and once again, my training regimen paid off. Otherwise, I would have been done.

The further I walked, the thicker the brush grew. I mustered enough strength to move onward, swatted mosquitoes the size of small birds and a variety of other flying bugs. Memories of the highland jungle crept into my thoughts. The alarm on my watch buzzed. I was behind my estimated time to walk a half mile.

The mountainside was thick with trees, vines, and the ground covered with tangled masses of briar patches. That made the trek slow and arduous. The map showed a small side trail that led down the slope to the cabin. I studied the surroundings and remained observant. Around two hundred yards further, I found the tree with a heart carved on it. I squatted through an opening in the briar patch that resembled a tunnel.

To get through, I low-crawled under limbs with thorns that grabbed at pant legs and shirt sleeves. Cacophonies of birds sent out warnings of my presence. Squirrels and rabbits jumped out of cover. I let out a sigh of relief that there were no boars or snakes. The crawling was slow, and the brush blocked most of the sunlight. I checked my watch; I was running short on time.

I kicked myself, thinking I should have waited until morning. Nevertheless, I wanted to get there before Cree. I had hoped he was not listening in real time. It may be later tonight when he checked the recording from his listening devices.

I tried to focus my eyes as far down the trail as possible, but the cabin was not in view. According to the map, I was close. A movement in the distance caught my eye.

On the other side of the briar patch, a black bear rummaged its nose through a piece of ground. I ignored the bear and turned my attention ahead. The weathered logs of a small cabin under a large crop of Ivy came into view. I inched my way towards the dilapidated structure. At the end of the briar patch, a thick layer of vines and ivy climbed tree limbs planted in the ground like poles.

I reached the unlocked cabin door. The rusted hinges squealed, and the foul smell hit me like a punch in the jaw. I turned on a small flashlight, and it revealed a scene shoddier than Sam described. Dew's small daypack, an unrolled sleeping bag, food wrappers, and cans were strewn everywhere on the dirt floor. Charred wood rested in the hearth of the stone fireplace. A kettle hung on the spit. The cabin smelled of must, wood smoke, and shit.

Piles of green mold covered the remains of a meal in a tin mess kit on the table. My light hit a dark red stain that looked like blood. Flies buzzed all around the blood and a hole dug in the far corner of the room for excrement.

On the other side of the table, a chair with bloodstained spindles and top rail laid on the dirt floor. A pool of caked blood had formed in a divot. Dew must have thrust his body backward, and the chair toppled over creating the divot.

I visualized the scene. Mason Dew sat at the table eating a meal.

Someone he knew and trusted had opened the door and walked inside. The person strolled over to the table and POW.

The reminder message ringtone on my cell dinged. "Dinner with Laura" appeared on the screen Laura got irritable whenever I was late. I pushed her name on the favorites list to call and explain. Nothing happened. There was no service.

Chapter 34

The headlights carved a path through the nightfall. The hike to the cabin and then back to the Explorer had taken longer than expected. My plan had been to get in and out before dark.

The V-8 roared to produce speed in the few short straight stretches, and the tires squealed through the curves. I knew driving this way was futile. I was already late for dinner. I glanced at my cell. Still no bars.

The trip wasn't a total bust. I didn't find the packets of Meth Reynolds mentioned. The blood evidence and Mason Dew's gear indicated the cabin was where Dew had stayed and probably where he was killed. Reynolds had implicated Officer O'Connor.

A loud bang reverberated through the cab. The Explorer lunged. The impact pushed my chest into the steering wheel; the cell sprung from my hand and landed on the passenger side floor. "Shit!" I yelled and grabbed the steering wheel with both hands.

The Explorer slid sideways. In a frenzy, I turned the steering wheel to compensate; the odor of burning rubber permeated the cab. Beams of light blinded me. Tapping the brake pedal, I managed to get the Explorer stopped sideways on the road. A loud airhorn blared. A huge slab of metal hit the driver-side door. My head snapped back when the side airbag deployed.

My confusion blended with the sound of crunching metal and shattering glass. The world turned upside down, rolling and bouncing. Brush and trees cracked and slapped the Explorer. The windshield was a cobweb of lines. The roof interior touched my head.

After what seemed like an eternity in a dryer drum, the vehicle came to a stop. I was conscious but dazed. *Laura is going to be mad as hell*, I thought. Everything hurt. I couldn't tell if anything was broken. The smell of gasoline triggered fear. My body strained against the seat belt. The Explorer had landed passenger-side down. In desperation, I released the seat belt.

I tried to cling to the back of the seat to ease my legs out first and stand on the passenger door, but I lost my grip and fell against the half deflated passenger side airbag. I felt around in the darkness for the cell. I checked my shoulder holster. The gun was still in place.

Lying on the passenger door, I felt like a pile of pulverized meat. My fingers found the cell phone.

I brought up the menu and turned on the flashlight app. Battery life was fifty percent, "I'm amazed it still works," I muttered. The inside of the Explorer was a mess. In another type of vehicle, I would have been dead.

I knew this wasn't an accident. Someone had pushed me over the edge. *Will they come down to check and make sure I'm dead?* The daypack in the back contained extra ammo clips. I figured I could pull myself sideways, slide over the center console between the bucket seats into the back seat, and then over the backseat to the cargo area. Every muscle in my body ached, and warm blood oozed from my nose. I struggled to think. My left leg burned like hell, and my vision was blurred. I felt like puking, but I was determined to get out alive.

Getting to the cargo area exhausted my strength. Lying on my back, breathing heavy, and holding my rib cage, I grabbed the daypack with the extra ammo clips, food, water, and the flashlight. The pain was almost unbearable; the gasoline odor grew stronger.

The person who ran me off the road may have been close. The Explorer could burst into flames at any moment. I slid back over the seats from the cargo area, hauling the daypack. Using the heel of my hand, protected by the nylon daypack, I hammered the glass until it gave way. Clearing shards of glass from the window frame, I climbed halfway out, unholstered my weapon. I couldn't see anyone and pulled myself outside. I sat on the doorframe with some relief. Rain began to patter on my head. "What will I do now?" I mumbled.

A large tree had stopped the Explorer's decent before it rolled over a cliff. I climbed out. My mind swirled, in the dark, my battered body worked through the pain. I dug in, clawing my way up the steep terrain. *Get away before it explodes.*

Chapter 35

I opened my eyes, "Hey—"

"Hey yourself, how do you feel?" Laura leaned over kissed my forehead.

"Sore. Where am I?"

"Blount Memorial Hospital. Do you remember what happened?" Laura prodded.

"I remember glancing at my cell phone, to see if I had any bars; to call and tell you I was late but on the way. A vehicle rammed the Explorer," I winced. Laura's fingers soothed me. "The Explorer slid sideways; I fought for control, blinded by headlights glaring off the mirrors. The side airbag deployed when a truck rammed the driver side door. I had a death grip on the steering wheel. My foot jammed down the brake pedal, and I heard the roar of a diesel engine. It pushed the Explorer across the road. Then it felt like I was in a dryer drum. I remember getting out, afraid the gasoline would explode in flames and nothing after that."

"Fortunately, the Explorer didn't catch fire. State Police believe the person who ran you off the road used a dump truck."

"I remember an air horn," I said. "Right before it rammed the door."

"What were you doing out on Route 107, Robert?"

"Checking out a cabin, way back in the woods, Sam said your dirty cop had used it for his meth lab."

"You mean Darrell? He had his lab in a mobile home not a cabin."

"Has Sam talked to you?" I said.

"No, he's been away from the office today. Why?" Laura said.

"Sam came to the house and said he suspected O'Connor was selling meth. He alleged O'Connor and Darrell had been working together with Mason Dew. Sam told me he had followed O'Connor to the cabin."

"What cabin, Bob? I have no idea what you're talking about."

"Sam drew a map to the cabin and I went there to check it out. The map's in my shirt pocket. How long do I need to be in here?"

"You will be with us overnight for observation Mr. Snow," the nurse said when she pulled the curtain back. She pushed a cart, with a laptop and other medical devices attached, close to the bed then she swiped a thermometer across my forehead.

"Why overnight?" I said.

"You have a concussion, cracked ribs, and sprained knee. The doctor ordered more tests."

"I've got things to do," I said.

"They will wait," Laura said. She unfolded the map, "Sam drew this?" I nodded. The nurse finished taking my vitals, recorded the numbers with her laptop, and then left the room.

"Sam, who by the way hates you, came to your house with information about another one of my officers being involved with the meth trade?"

"Yeah, it was strange. The first thing I asked him was if he talked to you. He said no. He didn't want to hurt you because O'Connor is your favorite." Anger flared in her eyes,

"I don't have favorites, and before you point to yourself, you don't work for me. Sam knows he can come to me, and he better have more than just a notion about O'Connor."

"I found the cabin, and like Sam said, Mason Dew's pack and camping gear were there. The table had a bloodstain on it, a mess kit with rotten food, a bloodstained chair was overturned, and blood pooled on the floor. I didn't stay in the cabin long. The hike through the woods and brush had taken longer than I expected. In many places, I had to crawl under the briar. It's hard to fathom a big man like Sam able to make that trek. You should inform the FBI. They may find the bullet that killed Dew in the cabin wall."

"I'll notify them, and I'm going to have a talk with Sam," Laura said.

"Be careful. He knew I would follow the lead he gave me."

"You think Sam is involved? Cree has your house bugged. He heard everything you and Sam discussed. Odds are better Cree ran you off the road."

"Or he alerted the police and told them where I could be found," I said.

"Could be, but for a guy who would like to see you dead—"

"If Cree kills me, his method will be neat and clean. He wants us to find this killer."

"On another note, while I was waiting for you I started to read The Badge of Deceit." She held the book so I could see the cover. "Didn't read the entire book, but the plot is a top level government project to create super-human warriors. I don't understand most of the stuff."

"That sounds far-fetched," I slurred.

"It sounds like science fiction, but Keefe was known to have inside information for all of her books. In this book, it's genetic manipulation. Are you listening?"

"Yeah, I heard you. Just tired—"

"I think the pain meds are kicking in." Laura kissed me, "I'll be in the recliner beside your bed," she whispered.

Chapter 36

The next morning I anxiously pushed away the breakfast tray. The shower had stopped, and the bathroom door opened. "Good morning," Laura said when she walked out toweling her hair.

"I'm ready to get outta here," I said. "Did you stay overnight?"

"Right there in the recliner."

"I want to stop and get a real breakfast," I said. "Afterward, I want to go to the scene."

"If you're up to it, we can also go over to the State Patrol Post and take a look at your Explorer," Laura said.

"I'll be up to it. Might be slow, but I'm not down for the count. Ribs hurt when I laugh or cough."

"You might be out of commission for a while," she said.

"Not unless you're in the mood to wrestle," I replied. While we were exchanging glances, a Tennessee Highway Patrol Officer walked through the door. He greeted Laura and me giving us his last name, Peterson.

"Mr. Snow, you look a lot better than the last time I saw you."

"I feel rough around the edges, but all in all, I'm doing well," I said. "Your techs looked over the Explorer yet?"

"They did. The initial impact was on the left side of the rear cargo door. That threw your vehicle into a spin. The vehicle that hit you had to be a large truck. Your Explorer went sideways, and the truck plowed you through the guardrail and over the edge, definitely was not an accident."

"You suspected a dump truck," Laura said.

"The markings on the Explorer lead us to determine it was a large truck with a snow plow attached," Peterson said.

"Can't be many of those around in July," I said.

"We're investigating this as an attempted homicide. The plow will have paint from your Explorer on the blade. You're fortunate you came out of that wreck alive, Mr. Snow."

"Thank you, Patrolman. Anything else?"

"A hiker found you and reported the accident from C.W. Grocery in Newport. It took the rescue team an hour to tend to your injuries then hoist you up the slope. It took half a day to get your Explorer out - what's left of it. Anyway, we'll continue to search for the suspect."

"Thanks, I will call my insurance adjuster." Peterson started for the door. Then he stopped and said,

"A woman showed up at the Post to see your Explorer. A writer. Her name was Thelma Burke."

"Thanks," I said.

Laura said, "Why would Thelma want to see Bob's SUV?"

"She told me she's doing research for a new book," Peterson said and left the room.

"If that's true, then we know who her prime suspect is." She laughed when I sighed.

"I should feel fortunate to be cast in one of her novels." I looked at Laura and said, "Why the long face?"

"Sam, he owns a dump truck. Hauls manure, and garden soil on the side."

"He has a snow plow on the truck?"

"I saw one last winter," she said. "The vehicle should be parked at his farm."

"So Sam told me the story about O'Connor to draw me out where he could run me over."

"Seems that way. I know Sam lied about O'Connor," Laura said. "At least I hope it was a lie. Hell, my whole department is out of control. First Darrell, now Sam is up to some kind of mischief."

"We don't know for certain Sam did this to me, Laura. If it does turn out that way, then it's best to get it busted up and dealt with. It's two cops, not the entire force."

"That's not comforting. There are nine cops on the force, not counting Sam and me. The Mayor and City Aldermen will crucify me."

"Could be worse," I said.

"Damn it Robert, how could it get any worse than that?"

"Under different circumstances, you would not have me here to help you."

Laura groaned. "We need to check out Sam's farm."

Chapter 37

After breakfast, Laura and I went to Newport. We wanted to question the person at C.W. Grocery who had seen the hiker. Peterson had given us a general description of a man that could fit anyone.

"Maybe Cree drove the truck." Laura said.

"I know you don't want it to be Sam, but running me over with a dump truck is not Cree's style," I said. "He's a gunman."

"Cree did threaten you outright and made an attempt on your life."

"Cree warned me about the surveillance on my house and helped me dispatch the shooters hiding in the woods. If he wanted me dead, I'd be dead already."

"Let me clarify, Robert. You think Cree helped you fight those gunmen, but you're not sure since Cree disappeared that night. The only evidence we found came from the insurgents and you. Cree left you there to die."

"Cree told me that the killer is closer than we think," I added. "The killer is someone we know." Laura's eyes saddened.

She blinked back a tear then said, "What possible motive would drive Sam to kill you?"

"Getting close to discovering his involvement in the Todd murder is one motive. Maybe he's the one who had been conspiring with Darrell. Sam gave me the heads up on the cabin. He knew I couldn't resist going up there."

"I still can't wrap my brain around it. I can't believe Sam tried to kill you," Laura said.

"Until we go to the farm and prove otherwise, I suspect Sam did."

"I can't believe it's Sam. He's got issues, but I can't believe he's a killer."

"I know. We take one step at a time."

Chapter 38

Laura pulled the unmarked car into the small parking lot at C.W. Grocery. We looked around at the few neighboring houses and a Holiday Inn across the street. The grocery sat a quarter mile from the I-40-exit ramp. Otherwise, there was not much else around.

"Don't forget your cane," Laura reminded me. I reopened the passenger door and retrieved the dreadful walking stick.

"Don't see why I need this when I can limp just fine."

"You know the doctor said it keeps you from losing your balance. It's temporary, old man," Laura chided.

Inside the market, we strolled to the manager's office. He greeted us with a hearty "Good morning."

"I'm Chief Bright, Winfield Creek Police Department. This is Robert Snow."

"How can I help you?" The manager said.

"We would like to talk to the person who spoke with the hiker the other morning," Laura said.

"Sure, that's me. I called the Newport Police when this fellow told me about the accident."

"What did he look like?" I asked.

"Tall, square jaw, rugged looking. I had been checking inventory, up front, when he rushed in out of breath. He had been running hard for quite a ways. I came back to my office to call the Newport Police. When I went back to the front, the man had left the store. He wrote down the directions to the wreck on a slip of paper and gave it to the cashier."

"Is that cashier working today?"

"Nope. Do you folks know who had the accident?"

"I did, and thank you for a quick response. I'd like to find the hiker, to thank him. Do you think he is from around here?"

"I've owned and operated this grocery for thirty years. Never seen the man before, and he had a yankee accent." We thanked the merchant and walked outside.

I said, "No cameras in the grocery or the parking lot, but from the description it could have been Cree. Once again he saved my life."

"I'll buy that until we know more. Never thought I'd be grateful he bugged your house," Laura said. A half hour later, we were standing on the curve where the truck rammed me. I peered over the bent guardrail and whistled. "Steep and a long way down."

"Lucky for you those big trees were grouped together, or the Explorer would have rolled to the bottom. Be hard to survive that. God's looking out for you, Robert."

"All I know is I'm fortunate." I walked back down the road looked at the skid marks from the Explorer going sideways and the wider tire marks made by a large truck.

"That hiker didn't just happen to find you," she said. "Look at the terrain on the other side. It is steep, no trails, and a rock cliff. No one would be coming down that way, and there are no trails on this side either." She looked back across the road at the rock face fifty feet straight up. "He had been searching for you, Bob."

"Jack Cree," I said. Laura nodded. "Hard to figure him out."

"Okay, let's head over to the State Police Post. We can get some lunch too. Then our last stop is Sam's farm."

"You're already hungry? You knocked down a big breakfast less than two hours ago."

"My body is healing. It needs plenty of fuel."

Chapter 39

The beaten up Explorer sat on a trailer in the impound lot when we arrived at the Highway Patrol Post. The extent of the damage shocked me. Lady Luck had been on my side. We walked to the office to ask for Peterson.

"Patrolman Peterson is working an accident. It may be a few hours before he can speak with you. I'll radio him," the young dispatcher told us. We could hear Peterson respond.

"Tell them we have no leads on the truck and driver. I will be another hour on the scene."

The dispatcher looked at us. "There is coffee and pastries if you want to wait."

"We can't wait. Coffee will be great," Laura said. The dispatcher brought coffee for Laura and for me a coffee and two pastries.

"Yuck—this coffee is thick as mud." Laura said after we were in the car.

"It's strong," I said through a mouthful of pastry.

Laura opened her car door, poured her drink on the pavement, and then said, "Next stop Sam's place."

Chapter 40

When Laura pulled onto the long gravel driveway at Sam's farm, it was late afternoon.

"I can't believe the big lunch you put away after eating most of the pastries at the Post," Laura said. "Your middle is starting to get pudgy."

"Two pastries. And my metabolism is sluggish since I haven't been able to run. Do you know where Sam is?"

"I sent him to J's Pizza do the follow-up report on a shoplifting case. He'll be tied up for a few hours."

"That should give us more than enough time to snoop around," I said.

"Or roll in the hay," she winked.

The peak of the traditional white two-story farmhouse and the red barn were visible from the road. The driveway was lined with tall pines. Hay fields stretched from the yard to the two-lane country road. Laura parked alongside the house with the car pointed towards the barn. "How much land does Sam have here?" I asked.

"A hundred and fifty acres," Laura said.

"How long had this been in Sam's family?"

"His great grandparents, I believe. Not sure how many other families had lived on this farm. This entire area was North Carolina's western land ceded to the Federal Government in 1789. Also, the Cherokee Nation comprised this area." It was easy for Laura to digress into the past.

"They were involved with Timothy Lyle's troubles as well. However, it doesn't help us now," she said.

"I know—Laura, if we find the truck and plow on this property, it won't do us any good. We don't have a search warrant."

"We don't have enough probable cause to get a search warrant. I need to know if Sam is guilty. We can piece the evidence together later," Laura snarled.

"He lives alone?" I asked overlooking her cantankerous tone.

"Yes, his mother lives in Nashville. Don't have a clue about his father, and there is a cemetery over there by the grove of apple trees." I looked out over the field to where Laura pointed.

"Sam has a beautiful place," I said, "Has he ever been married?"

"Not to my knowledge." We walked toward the large barn that sat to the left side and about fifty yards behind the house. The driveway extended to the barn and to an earthen ramp up to a set of large padlocked double doors. We walked around the side. The path led down a bank to a lower level door, locked from the inside.

"There's a barnyard door. It should be open," Laura said and climbed the board fence. As she stepped down, her feet sunk up to her ankles in cow manure.

"I would climb over too, but my leg…" I said lifting the cane.

"Yeah right, you city boys are afraid of a little cow poop," she said and sloshed through the mud and manure toward the rear of the barn.

It was the funniest scene I've ever witnessed.

"You owe me, Robert!" Laura shouted over a groan. A few minutes later, she slid the barn door open. She stood before me with her pant legs and western boots stained greenish-brown and dripping wet.

"Too bad we had a hard rain last night," I laughed.

"Just remember, you have to ride back with me."

The lowest level had three pens. Two were empty, and the one on the right held a large sow with a dozen piglets.

"And I thought the Bean Pot motel smelled bad," I said.

"Farm smell. Human smell is a lot worse. Come on. We have business to finish."

"I don't see a truck with a snow plow," I said.

"It wouldn't be down here. If Sam had a plow on that old dump truck it may be parked on the next level," Laura said, pointing up the ladder. "This is a hay chute it goes all the way to the top floor. The next level is where the large double doors were padlocked." I looked up the long dark vertical tunnel. Laura pushed past me and started to climb. The wood ladder had thin boards nailed on two-by-fours. The ladder was built onto the back inside wall of the chute was straight up. Manure fell off her boots on each rung. I hobbled as fast as I could to get clear, but particles of the smelly waste landed on my shoulders.

"What do I do?" I yelled up to her.

"Stay where you are. I'll take a look around." I found a hay bale and sat down outside the pigpen. Laura's footfalls drummed on the wood floor above. The sow snorted while her piglets sucked. The barn supports were rough wood beams about sixteen inches in diameter connected to cross-members with wooden pegs. I looked across the way to a closed door. I shuffled over and pulled the door open. The room contained two barrels of grain. On the sidewall hung harnesses, axes, hammers, a scythe, two shovels, and a long-handled tool I couldn't identify. It had an iron head with a spike on one side and a flat blade on the opposite end. "I suppose this is standard equipment on a farm," I muttered.

Several minutes later, Laura climbed down the ladder, "farm equipment stored up there, but not the dump truck."

"Where else would he have parked his dump truck?" I said.

"Let's go back outside. Maybe there's another outbuilding somewhere else on the property," Laura said.

"Good, the smell of pigs is getting to me. Are you going to wash off those cowgirl boots before we get in the car?"

"Maybe," she chuckled. We looked out across the green pasture and watched a herd of beef grazing. Then Laura pulled up a strand of barbed wire and climbed through.

"Are you coming?" she said and held the wire up. After several minutes of struggle, I tore through the small opening with the barbs catching my pants and shirt. Amid Laura's snickering, she scraped her boots against the grass and then we hiked to the apple orchard where the cemetery was located.

"This is an old cemetery," I said. "There are death dates from the early eighteen hundreds. The Reynolds' have a long history in Winfield Creek."

"That doesn't make sense. Sam told me his family was from Nashville. Sam's great grandparents lived here, but most of the family lived in Nashville. Sam's mother graduated law school in Nashville. Sam returned to Winfield, bought the old homestead, and joined the force."

"That's when his mother pulled strings to get him hired as a Detective," I said.

"What are you talking about, Robert? You think I accepted favors to hire Sam. That pisses me off." Laura gave me the look; I knew I had stepped on a land mine.

"Sam told me the Mayor forced you to hire him because his mother was a large contributor to the Mayor's campaign."

"He's a liar. I don't like the way this adds up. Sam and I have never been friends, but we have a professional relationship. I can't understand his reason to fabricate that story."

"We need to find out. It could explain his motive, why he killed Todd and his attempt on my life. Also, who killed Mason Dew and why?"

"That's easy; to keep his mouth shut," Laura said. "Don't forget your buddy Jack Cree either. He could leave behind all of this and made it look like Sam was the culprit."

"He's not my buddy. We also need to have another talk with Thelma Burke. I want to hear it from her mouth. Why she's interested in my wrecked Explorer."

"That reminds me. Have any idea when you will get another vehicle?"

"You tired of hauling me around?" I asked.

"No, but we can cover more ground by splitting up. I have another car you can borrow."

"Can borrow the Jeep?"

"Not on your life," she said and grimaced. "Whoever made the attempt on your life knows they didn't succeed and will try again. Don't want my baby getting scratched."

"Your baby," I chuckled.

"Besides, if we both get knocked off in one swipe who will solve the murders?" she asked.

"O'Connor," I said.

"He's good, but not that good. I'm the only one who drives Awesome."

"You named your Jeep Awesome?" I laughed.

"What's so funny? You're attached to that Explorer."

"Not anymore I'm not."

"Oh, now that she is banged up you just move on." Laura said, "You treat all your women that way?"

"The Explorer was not a living, breathing, person," I said.

"Coulda fooled me by the way you talk about that huge gas guzzler."

"That's not what I meant, Laura. You have another car at your place?"

"It's at my mamaw's house," Laura said.

"You're what?"

"Grandma, in your language," she said. "It's on our way. We'll stop and pick it up. By the way, can you drive a stick?"

Chapter 41

We arrived back at the station, after having a late dinner with Laura's grandmother. She served some of the best homemade apple dumplings I've had in my life. It had been years since I drove a stick shift. It showed. Car horns blared and people cussed at every red light and stop sign. I parked beside Laura's jeep. She smiled at me.

I had to crawl out from behind the steering wheel. "Never have I driven such a pink pile of junk."

"My college car and I've outgrown it. It used to have yellow daisy decals on the sides, but they had worn off."

"Lucky me," I quipped.

"Don't complain. Keep it as long as you like," she said.

"That won't be long. With sore ribs and a bum knee, it's difficult to pull me in and out of this metal shoe box."

"Oh how you complain, Mr. Snow," Laura said with an over exaggerated southern drawl.

"Hilarious," I said as we opened the glass doors to the station lobby. Norma smiled at us. "Like the little pink car, Mr. Snow." Laura laughed.

"It's a loan," I said, "and no, it's not my favorite ride."

"Any calls for me Norma?" Laura inquired.

"No calls. Mr. Snow, how are you feeling today?"

"Thank you for asking, Norma. I'm good." Laura glanced over the bullpen to Sam's empty desk. I followed her to her office, and she shut the door behind us.

"I'm exhausted, how about you?"

"We've had a long day." I said. Before I could sit down, my cell vibrated. "Private caller ID," I said. "Hello."

"It's time, Bob," Cree said.

I nodded to Laura and mouthed Cree to confirm the caller. "Time to talk," I said to Cree.

"Yes, walk out to the Beetle, drive north towards I-40. Bring your girlfriend. No one else."

"We've had a rough day, Jack."

"Just you and the Chief," Cree said. "First name basis, it seems we're becoming buddies, Bob."

"Well, you did save my life."

"Twice, Bob," Cree said and hung up.

Laura said, "What's that about?"

"We're going for a ride," I said. Laura walked towards her Jeep. "No," I said. "Let's take the Beetle."

"You're kidding!" Laura gave me the look.

"Cree said to drive the cute Beetle, probably because it sticks out, easier for him to follow."

"I'm driving," she said. "I don't need whiplash."

"Drive north." We pulled onto Main Street and towards I-40.

"Now what?" Laura said.

"We wait for another call, I think. What year is this Beetle?"

"Seventy-three, a classic," Laura said. "I bought it from an old man who had it stored in his barn. He was the original owner."

"Don't recall these cars coming in pink."

"I had it repainted. Back then I liked the color and needed to be different."

My cell chimed, "Cree." I put the phone on speaker.

"Drive West on I-40 and take the Lenoir City exit." The call dropped off.

"That's close to sixty miles. This will be an all-night expedition, Bob."

"What's in Lenoir City?" I wondered.

"A small town, it sits between Interstate I-75, and the Little Tennessee River."

"What is exceptional about Lenoir City?" I said.

"A small town growing up and I can't imagine why Cree wanted to meet there," Laura said.

"It's a long way from Winfield Creek. Maybe he felt more secure there." After an hour drive, we passed the route forty seventy-five split.

"Lenoir City is the next exit," Laura said.

My cell rang. "Next exit, Bob. Turn left. Drive to Broadway. Turn right. Pull over and wait for my call." Cree hung up.

Chapter 42

Laura took the exit and turned left. We crossed the highway bridge and pulled into the Texaco service station. "We need gas?" I said.

"No, this baby goes a long way on a tank. Further than I go. I need coffee and to go to the restroom."

"I better do the same," I said. While I was unpacking my body from the Beetle, my cell chimed "By the Seaside." "What!"

"You stopped. Why?" Cree said. I scanned the street and pump area trying to spot him. "Need to go to the bathroom and get some coffee. We've had a long day," I said.

"Make it quick."

"This is getting old fast," I grumbled, and then limped toward the men's room. Afterward, I purchased two hot coffees and returned to the car.

"Cree has eyes on us. He called and wanted to know why we stopped," I said. Leaning on the opened door of the Beetle, I handed Laura a coffee.

"I'm tired and out of patience. I don't like being jerked around," Laura said when I climbed in beside her. She took a slow sip of hot coffee. "Just what I needed."

She turned the key and stomped the accelerator, the four-cylinder engine whined as if in pain. The tiny car bolted in reverse with Laura whipping the wheel with one hand. She braked hard. I struggled to avoid burning my crotch with hot coffee. She moved her coffee cup to her left hand. My head jerked back when she shifted the Beetle around the gas pumps. Fortunately for us, business was slow. She guided the little car onto the road, with tires squealing. We sped down Route 321. Laura sipped coffee with her eyes dead ahead and ignored the posted speed limit.

"You're in a hurry!" I said.

"Like I said, I'm tired of being jerked around by this butt hole. We have more important things to do than massage his ego." I hummed agreement and enjoyed the coffee. We turned onto Broadway. Laura pulled to the curb. We sat still, with the motor idling.

"You changed my ringtone?" I asked.

"You needed an upbeat tune," she said. "You're depressed." I started to respond when Cree called. I put it on speaker.

"Drive to the 5th traffic light and turn right." Laura pulled away from the curb. Cree continued talking, "go up and over the hill to 6th avenue, and then turn left. At the 3rd stop sign is C Street, turn right and then a left onto 7th Street."

"Wait—what are you trying pull, Cree?"

"Shut up Bob, and follow directions. The first stop sign is E Street take a right. Around the second bend is a small house on the right with an orange light in the window. Turn down the driveway and pull up beside the little barn in the rear of the house." Cree clicked off.

"Got all that?" I asked. Laura nodded.

"This is weird, Bob. I feel like we're driving to an ambush."

"And no one else knows where we are," I replied.

"A lot of good it would do if they did. Don't think I can count on Sam anymore." Laura followed Cree's directions with my help and turned down the small driveway. She slowed the car to a crawl. We had our weapons ready, and my head pivoted side to side looking for movement. We did not see Cree and stopped beside the front of the old barn. It was a tiny barn. Actually, I'm not sure it qualified as a barn. It was more like a large shed. Laura killed the engine. I jumped at the sound of a knuckle rap on the window. Cree stood pointing a rifle toward my head. He motioned with the barrel for us to get out.

"Keep your hands where I can see them." We climbed out of the Beetle, our eyes locked on Cree.

"We come in peace," I said.

"If you tipped off anyone where you are, you're both dead."

"We didn't tell anyone," Laura said.

"You didn't have to bring us all the way out here to execute us, Jack."

"Bob, don't be so dramatic. You will get your chance to be the hero for your little woman another day. Pop the trunk and stow your weapons." We laid our arms in the trunk, and before Laura could close the lid, Cree said, "your knife also, Bob. Securing your weapons is for my safety."

"You're the one with the rifle," Laura said. The full moon cast an eerie light on the scene, the three of us stood outside the small windowless weather-worn barn. I looked past Laura to the house with the orange light in the window,

"Anyone live up there?" Cree didn't answer and pointed us toward the side of the barn. He opened a door, and we stepped through the narrow passage. Cree closed the door. He turned the light on. The glow from the bug light bulb cast a yellow hue over the room.

"This is where I tell you both what's going on in Winfield Creek. You'll thank me in the morning," Cree said.

"We're listening," Laura said.

"For starters, I reiterate I did not kill anyone in Winfield Creek." I gave him a frown. "Not even those thugs who were camped outside your house, Bob."

"You left me!"

"You're still alive," Cree chuckled. "You're such a boy scout. 'I only kill in self-defense' you had said. All I did was to give you the chance to deal them on your terms."

"Did you know who they were?"

"They work for Cyberhound," Cree said.

"Never heard of it,"

"So how do you know about them?" Laura asked.

"I operate in a small world," Cree replied.

"Why would they hire a gunman to kill you?" I asked.

"They are in the software business, but not just any software. They deal with software bugs. They call them Vulnerabilities. That's not all they do."

"Jack, you brought us all the way out here to talk about software?"

Cree said, "This is a safer place for me. Software bugs are vulnerabilities exploited to hack into computers. We're talking about millions of dollars. Cyberhound finds bugs in software programs, checks them to determine if they are exploitable. Then sell them to our government and to other clients on the Dark Web, those who can afford them. Their largest customers, outside of NSA and CIA, are China, Russia, and a host of other European countries. The vulnerabilities are used to gain access to computer networks so they can disrupt activities and steal secrets."

"So that's why NSA is involved." I said.

"They were the first to buy an executable bug back in the eighties. My orders were to retrieve the hard drive from Todd's house. The disk contained software bugs that belonged to the agency. These vulnerabilities are the bullets in cyber warfare," Cree said.

"This is a little over my head," I said. "So, are you about to tell us Marilyn was killed for the hard drive that contained these bugs?"

"I didn't kill her, and neither did Keefe."

"How can you be sure she didn't kill her?" I said. "And how do you know Monica Loves' real identity?"

"We worked together on many cases. An excellent asset, but she liked boys too much."

"She was a pedophile?" Laura reacted with disgust.

"Not like that," Cree said. "Young men, like the Farber kid. Of course, I had been her inside informant, back when I worked for the Bureau. Things got hot for her so she dropped off the grid. We reconnected; she wanted me to teach her how to hide. She wrote about government conspiracies, and she wanted firsthand experience with how assassins operated."

"So, you taught her some tricks of the trade," I said. "What got her killed?"

"She saw your killers."

"You mean there were more than one involved with Todd's murder?" Laura's tone revealed her skepticism with Cree's answer.

"I tried to tell her to stay clear of Farber. He would get her exposed. She wouldn't listen."

"The morning of Todd's murder, Monica—uh Elaine -ran from the house and Dew saw her," Laura said.

"She wanted to do the break-in," Cree replied. "To get the hard drive. She got in just fine, but when she saw the two come out of the upstairs bedroom, she panicked and bolted out the door."

"Mason Dew was across the street," Laura said.

"That's right, and he gave her description to the police."

"Did you kill Dew?" I questioned.

"No, I had my own problems with my employer. Dew wasn't worth my time."

"You also have problems with the FBI," I said.

"They want me for a different reason. The NSA contracted a lot of work my way."

"Hold on a minute," Laura interrupted. "Did Love…I mean Keefe give you descriptions of the two coming from Todd's bedroom?"

"Too dark inside the house to see features, but the one thing she believed was one of them was a man, tall and big." I sensed the wheels turning in Laura's head.

"What did she say about the second person?"

"Nothing, too hard to see and she got out of there fast. When Elaine failed to get the hard drive, I waited until things cooled down then entered the house to get it myself. The night I kicked your ass, Bob." He smiled, and I cringed. "After looking at the files, I figured the contents of the drive got Todd killed."

"I found the expected bugs on the drive and another file. I read and copied it before turning the hard disk over."

"The NSA discovered you had accessed the file?" I said.

"The file confirmed the truth about the subject of Elaine's last book. The one book I did not collaborate with her on." Cree paused. We remained silent and waited for Cree to continue. "I believe Todd had been Elaine's source for that book. After I had read the file, it dawned on me the file is what Elaine wanted. She needed to retrieve it to have proof of her claims in the book."

"What's in the file?" I asked.

"Along with documents, the file contained a map of a place the government will go to any length to keep secret. The text is a report on the progress of a black ops program that started at the end of World War II. Government scientists had been conducting experiments on human embryos, and that progressed to genetic engineering."

"I read most of the book. It seemed unbelievable," Laura said. Cree continued,

"A select group of government scientists continued Hitler's eugenics program to build the master race. However, not in the area of ethnicity as Hitler desired. The government had been engineering assassins and politicians." I heard Cree's voice, but my mind was numb, and I felt shocked with disbelief.

"Really! The government!" Laura yelled. She stared at Cree.

"People in the government—rouge bureaucrats, hell I don't know!" Cree shouted in defense.

"Let's calm down," I intoned.

"This is what's in the file. It does not mean the data is authentic. All I know is what I read," Cree said. "Elaine never mentioned any of this to me."

"Does it say how they tested subjects?" Laura asked.

"The report listed dozens of NSA sponsored adoption centers." Laura's face froze with an angry scowl.

"The thought of those innocent babies tampered with in the

womb," she said.

"This does sound like a wild fantasy, Jack," I said.

"I know it sounds crazy, but it's probable. We both know there are those in the government who believe they are gods."

"That is a strange accusation from a hired assassin," I said.

"Another part of the file listed names," Cree continued. "Many are still working for the CIA, FBI, NSA, MI, and I recognized names of a few men and women in Congress and a couple of past Presidents. Marilyn's name was recorded in the donor column. They wanted her babies."

"That would answer the question why she needed to hide, but why in Winfield Creek?" I was puzzled.

"I found two other familiar names on the list, Bob." Cree watched my reaction. Then he said, "My name is listed. I was genetically altered."

"You're insane."

"Yeah, and he has the rifle," Laura said.

"GAP, Genetically Altered Person."

"Who's the other?" I said.

"You," Cree said. "You and I are siblings." The shock from his words staggered me.

"How can you say that?" I demanded.

"It's in the file. I made a copy. I think Elaine had figured it out too." He handed me a thumb drive. "Here's a copy for you." I pocketed the device.

Laura turned to me and said, "Bob, we don't know if this is truth or some concocted fantasy by this lunatic."

"No, we don't!" Cree and I studied one another.

"Why did you bug my house?"

"To keep tabs on you and I needed your help, Bob."

"When you shot at me, on the mountain, you missed on purpose. Because you believed we're brothers," I said.

"No, I did not know then. After I had recovered the hard drive, it took me several hours to break the encryption. Along with killing people, I also have a skill set in cryptology. Yeah, I wanted to kill you years ago, but that day on the mountain, I wanted to draw it out. Savor your downfall. When I read the file, it shocked me to the bone. Like what you're feeling now, but the facts were our parents had been breeders for the government."

"It's a good story. It gives you a reason to get invested in my life."

"I don't believe any of this horseshit," Laura said.

Cree said, "Believe it or not. Another fact, you have two unsolved murders on your hands. I hope, Chief Bright, you're not going to accuse Elaine of killing Todd."

"Then tell me who the hell killed her!" Laura screamed.

"Anger won't help. Take the blinders off Chief. It was somebody you know. Bob, after you look at the file, you will understand," Cree said.

"Elaine had been your friend. The least you can do is to help us get the person who killed her." Laura interjected.

"I would like to, but I have other problems to solve. I can tell you that Todd worked for NSA, and her job was to purchase the bugs for the agency's use. She fell out of favor when she stole the black ops file."

"Why did she steal the file in the first place?" I asked.

"Because she got pregnant," Laura said. "My bet the father's a high ranking official in the NSA, married and Marilyn had been his side action."

"Makes sense to me," Cree said. "Still, no respectable assassin kills like a bloodthirsty lunatic. If my employer wanted Todd dead, that would have been my assignment and done neat and clean. Without the file, there is no proof of any covert programs. They wanted her babies. Therefore, someone else killed Todd for a different reason than the one Elaine had."

"Your employer discovered you had teamed up with Elaine," I said. "And they knew she wasn't Monica Love so they had her taken out. No more books." Cree shrugged that theory off as nonsense. "Where do you go from here?" I asked him.

"Wherever this information in the file takes me. I need to know if I am who I am or it's because some lab geek made me this way."

I didn't get the chance to respond. Cree stepped backward, opened the door pushing with his back, and then fled. By the time I hobbled to the opening, he was lost in the darkness.

"Such an odd man. Cree does not know the identities of the killers or he would have told us. We're right back where we started," Laura said.

"Maybe not," I added. "He said the killer is someone you know. Who else would be interested in such a wild tale?" Laura shrugged.

"Elaine Keefe, whom we knew as Monica Love, wrote books

about government conspiracies. And a genetic engineering program was the subject of her last book. She wanted the file and so, who else, other than the NSA, might be interested in the same information?"

"What are you thinking?" Laura asked.

"I'm not sure, but I want to talk to Thelma again. She knew more about Marilyn than she told us. I know what Jack said, but there's no way on earth we're brothers."

"When you access the thumb drive, you may have a different conclusion," Laura said.

"No, it's too easy to fake documents. I don't trust Cree. I wish I could figure out his end game."

"I haven't entirely ruled him out as the killer. All of this could be an elaborate ruse to get us off his trail," Laura said.

Chapter 43

Laura drove back the same way we came. We rode in silence. When we were near the Texaco, she downshifted, and pulled onto the I-75 ramp going east. She smashed the pedal to the floor. After she had throttled the Beetle up to cruising speed, I broke the silence, "You believe Cree fed us a load of bull."

"Don't know for sure, but right about now I would like to curl up and hope everything is clearer in the morning."

"I like your escapist approach, once in a while, but it won't solve this problem," I said.

"Which part of Cree's story do you think is bullshit, the bugs or the genetic engineering stuff?" Laura asked.

"I'm not savvy with computers," I said. "I have enough skill to use the things for simple tasks. Software bugs and cyber warfare is way beyond my knowledge. Using them for covert opportunities seems reasonable. On the other hand genetic engineering to create super humans is pure science fiction."

"You read Sci-Fi," she said. "The books are on your shelf. Space travel, once science fiction, is now science fact."

"I've seen a lot of strange things working for the government. The bugs I can believe genetic engineering, no. It gave Cree a plausible explanation to claim we are brothers, which is even more farfetched. I can't stomach the thought."

Laura glanced at me then turned her eyes back to the road ahead. She said, "I can see a resemblance." My face flushed. She grinned, and we ended up laughing at the outrageous thought.

When we caught our breath, "Tomorrow we need to have a good talk with Sam. He needs to explain a few things."

"I agree, he needs to explain the story he told you about the cabin and tell us where he parked his dump truck," Laura said.

"And the matter of running me off the road," I replied. "We need to revisit Thelma also. Who was the Officer Sam busted for selling Meth?"

"Darrell Lancaster—"

"How did you find out about him?" I asked.

"We received an anonymous tip. Sam started following Darrell and found his lab. Sam tried to arrest him. Darrell resisted and pulled his weapon. Sam killed him."

"How convenient," I said.

"Sam hasn't gotten over it. They had been friends for years."

"You just have Sam's word about Darrell?" I pondered.

"I arrived at the scene, Darrell's body on the ground outside of his mobile home, his service revolver beside him. The meth lab was inside his mobile home. Until now, I've had no reason to doubt Sam's account of the incident.

"We need to go there, and take a look around before we talk to Sam," I said.

Chapter 44

The following day, at the station, Reynolds went about his work. We had to force ourselves to act normal. Reynolds made some minor comments to me about my injuries, but he didn't inquire about the trip to the cabin. Laura pretended to be working the case all the while watching Reynolds.

After a light dinner at the Grinder, we rode out to Darrell Lancaster's place.

"Today has been the most miserable day of my life," Laura said. "I didn't want to talk to Sam, and when I had to, I felt like ripping out his eyeballs." She paused to take a few deep breaths. "Darrell's parents passed away several years ago, leaving him the homestead. He didn't have siblings."

"Who is mowing the yard?" I asked.

"Sam takes care of the place. His farm is straight across the hill from here," Laura said.

"Why is Sam the caretaker?"

"With no known next of kin, Sam purchased the house from Darrell's estate, about an acre of land," Laura said.

"Doesn't appear like much of an investment without the house being rented," I said.

"He made a sentimental purchase."

"Let's take a look inside that trailer," I said.

"Mobile home," Laura corrected. "It's locked and I don't have the key."

"That's not a problem," I said holding up a set of picks.

Laura frowned. "I don't want to see this," she said. "Make it quick." She turned with her back to me. In less than a minute, we were inside.

I clicked my pen light. "How long ago did Darrell have his lab here, Laura?"

"Two years ago."

"Who did the clean up?" I inquired.

"Sam had a company do it. Don't recall the name."

"Meth labs have a distinctive odor that can percolate in the walls for years. Need to get this place tested. I'm willing to bet we won't find any trace of Meth or any of the chemicals used to make it." I looked to Laura, "It is a possibility Sam staged the lab and the resisting arrest to get rid of Darrell."

"That's a hard thing to say, Robert. Damn, if Sam did that, it would tear this town apart. Everyone liked Darrell. Many people couldn't believe he was a drug dealer," Laura said.

"I will call Jon Pate, my Bureau contact and ask him to have an FBI lab technician check this place. In the meantime, how do we keep this from Sam?"

"Keep what from Sam?" We spun around. Reynolds stood outside the door with a shotgun trained on our chests.

"Don't try anything foolish, Agent Bob. This has two barrels, one for you, and one for the Chief."

"Sam, how do you expect to get away with killing us?" Laura's tone carried a pronounced defiance.

"I won't kill you, Chief. Agent Bob is going to do that. After all, he did kill Todd and Love. I arrived after he killed you, and I killed Agent Bob in self-defense. Everyone in town, including the Mayor, believes Agent Bob is our killer."

"Why did you kill Darrell, Sam?" I inquired.

"You expect me to just talk?" he laughed, "why not? You won't be able to tell anyone. He discovered my little secret. I couldn't let him spoil everything. Then, I rigged a meth lab in here, stocked with the right chemicals, of course. I handed him his weapon so he could defend himself, except it wasn't loaded, my bad."

"Well, that was an easy confession. I guess we can all go home now," I said sarcastically. "You believe you will get away with this, Reynolds?"

"I've gotten away with murder before. Twenty years and never caught, not even close," he snickered. "Now toss your weapons on the floor and walk towards me." We complied, and Sam turned on a bright mag light that blinded us. The light forced us to look down. Sam marched us towards the house. I looked for an opportunity to make a move, but if I did and he fired the double barrel, it would cut us in half. I limped along, wishing I had not left the cane in the car.

"Sam, how did you know we were out here?" Laura asked.

"Agent Bob's phone: you had me issue it to him and I set it up so I could track it. I knew that you two were together ninety-five percent of the time. So, odds were in my favor to get you both at my choosing." Sam chuckled and prodded us through the door and to the other side of the kitchen. "Open the cellar door, Agent Bob."

"I told you before, it was Special Agent." Sam pushed us, and we tumbled down the steep wooden steps. Bouncing off each other, we landed at the bottom in a pile. The floor was hard-packed dirt, damp and musty. Hitting the dirt floor was not much better than falling on concrete.

"You feel special now?" Sam yelled, and slammed the door putting the cellar in total darkness. I heard the bolt lock. My leg and ribs screamed with pain. Laura moaned.

"Are you okay?" I asked.

"Hell no, I'm not okay! What's that god-awful smell?" Laura inquired. "Why didn't Sam kill us outside?"

"Don't know, but I won't complain about that. We're alive, and it may give us time to find a way out of this place."

"You don't sound real optimistic," Laura said. I scrounged around until I located my pen light.

"You look beaten up," I said, shining the light on her face.

"I am beaten up and pissed off. Get that thing out of my eyes; use it to find a way out of here." I shined the light up the stairwell. The foul odor in the cellar caused my chest to tighten. The stairwell had no handrails, and the walls were level with the first riser.

"We're lucky we didn't fall off the side of the stairs," I said. I stood, holding onto a stair for balance. My leg was throbbing but did not feel broken. My ribs ached. "I have had more close calls with death working this case than all of my years in CID."

I inched my way up the stairs to the door. My head spun, my stomach rolled, and bile collected in the back of my throat.

"No key hole. The door is hard as oak," I shouted down to Laura. "It is bolted on the other side." I sat down on the top step and scooted down one-step at a time. The cellar was a damp black hole.

"We can't get out through the door, Laura. Can you move?"

"Slowly, I'm pretty beat up."

"No broken bones?" I asked.

"Just my pride," she said and took my hand. We felt our way along the cinder block wall; by the position of the stairs, we reasoned it was the front of the house. The pen light didn't illuminate a wide path. We were looking for another door or windows to the outside. I didn't expect to find any, but we had to rule it out.

We traversed from wall to wall until we got back to the steps. The area was twenty paces in length and ten in width. Neither windows nor another door existed. My penlight was fading. Near the center, we moved hand in hand slowly to the first support post. At the second support post, the earthen floor felt slippery, slimy, I thought to myself. I fanned the pen light to my right. There was an old coal furnace. "We can't climb up through that thing either. The duct work is too small," I said.

"Duh," Laura surprised me with her uncharacteristic schoolyard slang. "Ouch," Laura exclaimed. Chains rattled, sending an eerie chill down my spine. I shine the penlight towards her. A block and tackle hung from the load-bearing beam.

"What the hell!" she said. "Why are these chains hanging here?"

I shined the light down at our feet. Dark red stained the dirt floor. "Blood," I said.

The chain had blood on it too. Laura looked stricken. Her voice crackled. "This is a kill room," she said. I shined the light on the opposite wall. There were patches of dried blood splatter from hard blows to a human body. I staggered. My body stiffened. Laura felt the jerk, and she yanked my hand,

"Robert! Are you okay?"

"Give me a minute." I worked to steady my breathing, and then we moved back to the steps where we sat down to rest.

"I'm a lousy Chief of Police," Laura complained. "A detective who is a killer and I had no clue."

"Don't beat yourself up. No one else knew either."

"I think Darrell knew, and it got him killed," she said. "Like us."

"We're not dead yet," I said. I pulled open the pouch in my trousers and retrieved the stiletto. "Good thing Sam didn't search us," I said. "We can't escape. We wait, and when Sam returns we spring a trap." I removed my shirt and signaled for Laura to remove hers.

"Excuse me! No way am I going to be found dead with my boobs hanging out."

"The plan is not to die. I need the shirt to make a rope." Mumbling under her breath, Laura handed me her shirt. My hands trembled tying one sleeve from each shirt together and then wound them tight like a rope.

"Don't know what you're worried about. You have a bra on. We hide and when Sam comes down the steps. We yank the shirt-rope up and trip him."

"Nice payback for throwing us down those stairs," Laura smirked.

"It will take more than the fall to get him. Sam is big and stout. It will take both of us to overpower him. I have the stiletto to finish him off if it comes to that."

"Damn straight," she said. We worked to position our shirt rope and tested it. "This will work, Bob."

"We don't want to kill him. Knock him unconscious, and then we get help."

"At this point my brain says kill the traitor," Laura said, and we settled back to wait. Our trap was set at the fourth step; it was as high as we could reach. "Hope the fall will—" Laura whispered under her breath. We settled in behind the staircase.

"You need to get counseling." Laura whispered.

"What do you mean?"

"You know what I'm saying, Bob."

"No," I said, "I can cope."

"Suppressing the memories won't help."

"Since the wreck, I haven't been able to run. Letting it all hang out at angry rock was my therapy."

"Try prayer," she said. "I know you're not religious, and I'm not a regular church-goer either, but prayer helps."

"It's been my experience that most people are quick to turn to God when they are in trouble," I said. Laura dropped the subject, and we waited in silence. I had trouble keeping my eyes open. We had been working around the clock. Laura nudged me. A few hours in the cellar felt like days. "He's coming," Laura whispered.

"About time," I said. The sound of the bolt and the cellar door opened. A beam of light from the kitchen covered the upper half of the steps. Sam hesitated at the top. Did he hope to find us dead at the foot of the steps? I wondered and worried he would discover our trap. My adrenaline pumped in anticipation of the coming fight.

"Hey down there," Sam shouted. *Come on down, big boy*, I thought. Sam stood there shining his flashlight from side to side. From the doorway, he had a narrow view of the cellar.

"Now my darlings, where are you hiding?" Sam intoned in a high-pitched voice, mimicking a young girl. I wondered if he had an alternate personality. The wood creaked when Sam shifted his weight and stepped down then stopped on the first step. He hesitated on the step above the trap for more than a minute. *Come on, Sam.* I prodded with telepathy.

He stooped and panned his light. We slid further back. That

prevented us from keeping a grip on shirtsleeves, but we were still within reach to spring the trap. It would take precise timing for us to grab the shirt rope and yank it taunt. This plan had to work. We did not have a backup plan.

I reached over, found Laura's hand, and clutched it. I put my mouth to her ear and whispered for her to make the move when I tugged her hand.

Sam stood on the top step for a long time. Finally, impatience took over, and he jumped to the next step. His quickness caught us off guard, but we had time to grab the sleeves and yank. The shirt-rope sprang up. Taut, it caught one foot and sent Sam headfirst down the steps.

He bellowed. The impact of Sam's massive body shook the steps. I thought they might collapse. We rolled out from behind the stairs. A sudden flash of blue light blasted, and thunder deafened my ears. Sam had managed to fire the double barrel before he lost his grip and the shotgun fell over the side of the stairs.

"Laura, find the shotgun," I yelled and raced to where Sam laid. Adrenaline made my brain forget sore ribs and an injured leg. The light from the kitchen outlined his body, and I piled on driving an elbow into his back. Out of control, I continued to attack him with one fist while reaching for the stiletto with the other hand.

"I found it," Laura said. Sam didn't resist. I felt for a pulse.

"Sam's dead, Laura. She crawled over to my side and laid the shotgun down. The kitchen light cast a solemn glow over Laura's strained face. I pulled on Sam's body, and his head moved in the awkward motion of a broken neck. Laura bent over his body and wept.

Chapter 45

We spent most of the day at the Lancaster house huddled in the living room. The FBI had taken our statements. The state and Bureau forensics teams were working together collecting evidence in the cellar, and agents were searching the first and second floors.

"Jon, you came all the way from D.C. to work this case?" I inquired.

"Temporary transfer to Knoxville. Elaine Keefe raised a red flag. Jack Cree, also known as Ryan Keith was FBI. I was intrigued by Marilyn Todd's background. Furthermore, I hunt serial killers. And if it's true, what Sam told you about him killing for twenty years, when we get done processing this place and his farm; we may close a lot of cold cases."

"Twenty years, never caught, not suspected. That's the way Reynolds had put it. You may have cases you didn't know existed."

"He's done now, and I'm glad this killer has come to his end," Jon said. "Saves us a lot of time and the taxpayers' money."

"After all of the years of killing, it ends like this," I marveled. "He didn't kill us outright. Instead, he shoved us in the kill room. Why?"

"He waited until he had the time to savor the kill and then clean up. His knowledge of police procedure had helped him to avoid detection," Jon said.

"Sam told us that Darrell found out his secret. How do you suppose he discovered Sam was a killer?"

"Serial killers are not ordinary people, but they play the part extremely well to conceal their true nature. He must have slipped up and made Darrell suspicious. Sam's killing has come to an end. That's what counts."

"At least Darrell Lancaster's name will be cleared," I said. "This mess was tough on Laura."

"She seems like a strong woman," Jon said.

"She is, but what bugs me is why he killed Todd and Love."

"They likely fit a profile," Jon said. "We will build the profile and then we will know. You and Laura go home. Get some rest." Laura walked over and grasped my hand.

"Let's get out of here, go somewhere, and chill," she said.

"Sure, that sounds great," I said. "Let's go to my place. I'll fry up steak and eggs."

"Comfort-food," she said. We walked towards the Beetle.

"You know there's probably someone else out there," I said.

"Why?" Laura said, opening the car door and climbing into the driver's seat.

"Sam snatched his victims and took them to the kill room. His MO changed with Todd and Love. Why?" Laura hurried the Beetle out the driveway.

She said, "I don't know, but I'm tired and hungry, and it's hard to think about it."

"This case is a carousel that goes around and around—"

"We grabbed the brass ring today," said Laura.

"I wonder," I replied. Laura was silent as we sped down the country road towards home.

The speed limit drive to my front door was thirty minutes, and Laura had cut the time in half. She said, "I told you I was hungry." I started the grill for the steaks and pulled out the egg carton. Laura made the coffee. "One thing about Sam. He was a perfectionist at keeping accurate and precise records. Sam may have notes or documents about his exploits hidden somewhere," she said.

"Good thought. Serial killers have huge egos," I said. "It makes sense he would have the scheme to publicize his crimes. He certainly was quick to confess to us what he did. His reign lasted twenty years. Sam Reynolds, the serial killer, went unnoticed and unseen. He likely wanted an outlet to flaunt his self-proclaimed genius. Nevertheless, he remained silent. The steaks are almost done. Eggs coming up."

"I like steak medium and eggs over hard."

"Pink but no blood," I said.

"You know, eating this heavy is going to make it hard to sleep."

"After what we've been through, we need the nourishment," I smiled and lifted the steak and eggs to her plate. We ate with the gusto of starvation and then lay side-by-side on the couch with the empty plates on the floor.

Chapter 46

The morning light hit my face. I was groggy. My first thought was that the previous day had been a nightmare. Laura groaned and stretched. The bruises on her arms and face dispelled that theory. I gingerly leaned over and kissed the top of her head. "We slept all night and almost all day." I unwound my stiff and sore body from Laura's arms and legs. I picked up the plates and limped to the kitchen.

"I have this feeling—" I said from the kitchen, "—maybe something Cree said. He had been Keefe's inside snitch for her books.

"Except on the last book she wrote," Laura said and wrapped her arms around my waist, laid her head on my back while I rinsed the plates. She sniffed.

"What?"

"The garbage stinks," she said.

"I'll take it out in a moment. Cree thought Todd had stolen the file on the government's genetic design program for that book. What if Reynolds had a similar device to reveal his exploits?"

"Wait a minute; you said Cree lied about the program."

"I'm still not sure what to think. Let's say, for arguments sake, it's all true. It got me to thinking about a way Sam could massage his ego, through books. If he wrote under a pen name, his identity would be secret. He was confident of his genius because the police didn't know he existed."

"You mean like acting out a character in a novel?" Laura said.

"More like, he's the author and the main character. Readers believed the crimes committed were fiction, but in reality, they were truth."

"That would be a twist," Laura said. She removed her arms from my waist and opened the garbage canister.

"Another what if, Keefe didn't stop writing. She could have written some good crime novels under another name with Cree providing the police procedural element."

"Let's say you're on the right path," said Laura. "How did they know about Sam when no one else knew about his killing sprees?"

She opened the kitchen door and took out the garbage.

"I knew if I waited long enough you would take that out." She balled her fist and teasingly tapped my shoulder. "Darrell discovered Sam's secret life. Cree is an ex-FBI agent and contracts to NSA. He hunts down people for a living. It wouldn't be hard."

"Well, if Cree knew, he should have just told us and not let us get dragged through hell."

"I'll stay close to Jon and see what his team discovers at the farm," I said. "The more we know about Sam, the closer we get to understand his motive."

"You have that look. What else are you thinking?" Laura queried.

"Thelma writes crime fiction." Laura shot a look at me.

"Leave no stone unturned, Laura."

"I know, but Thelma and Sam didn't get along. I don't know what started it, but Sam had no use for Thelma Burke."

Chapter 47

"Hello, Bob."

"Cree, or should I say, Ryan Keith, why are you calling me? I'm busy removing the listening devices you planted in my house."

"Give me a break. I know you removed them right after I left you two in the barn. Keith was my alias at the bureau. I called to congratulate you for knocking off the killer."

"How did you work for the FBI under a false name?"

"Let's just say my resources have deep pockets."

"The bureau is not keeping your aliases a secret."

"I called to congratulate you, and you're giving me the third degree. Bet Laura is still wondering what happened to her police department," Cree laughed. "By the way, nothing has changed between us. You want to take me down to clear Colbert's record. I still have the false evidence to pin it on you. Stalemate. Did you look at the jump drive?"

"Not yet. Too busy trying to stay alive," I replied. "I don't believe what you said is true."

"Which part? The government programs or we're brothers?"

"Both," I said. "And I don't believe mom and dad were involved either. I think you fabricated the whole story and created documents to support it."

Cree heckled, "What's my motive?"

"That I haven't worked out yet."

"You're wrong Bob." Cree's voice softened his words tailed off. *The manipulator*, I thought, *trying to evoke sympathy*.

"Remind me, Jack or Ryan—whatever your name is, why did you call?" My tone sent the message: I'm tired of playing games.

"I wanted to congratulate you and Laura for ridding the world of one more prolific serial killer. Sam killed my beloved Elaine," Cree said.

"You loved Elaine, even though she preferred the young stud, David Farber, over you."

"Ah—you won't make me angry with that light jab. I forgave her many times for many assignations. Elaine had an insatiable hunger. Read what's on the drive. Face the truth. Goodbye, brother." The call dropped. I walked to the secretary and picked up the thumb drive a pang of dread floated in my stomach. I stared at the drive a full minute and then laid it down. *I'm not ready to deal with this. Not yet.*

Chapter 48

I walked into the Grinder, scoped out the other patrons, and then sat down with Charley.

"Glad you invited me to lunch, Robert."

"No problem, it's been a while, how are you doing?"

"I'm doing well. Heck of a thing about Sam, I imagine Laura's taking it hard."

"She's taking it in stride considering—how well did you know Sam?"

"We were not friends, but acquaintances. I am not sure anyone, other than Darrell Lancaster, called Sam a friend. Sam had always been hard to get to know. Folks are in a state of shock, though. Winfield Creek has become a murder capital. It worked out for you. Most people no longer believed you killed Marilyn Todd."

"That's something. Maybe in time, I will fit in around here. We still don't know why Sam killed Marilyn and Monica. The FBI Evidence Response Team Unit is still processing Sam's farm. So far, they have uncovered several skeletons. They found a kill room in Sam's barn. It was a subterranean room beneath a hog stall. They have found records in the house." I paused for the waitress. She took our orders. Then Charley asked,

"What type of documents?"

"Don't know about all of them, but some documented how he selected his victims and detailed how they were killed. Jon Pate invited Laura and me to a meeting this afternoon to share the details with us."

"Jon Pate?"

"Jon is my friend at the FBI," I said. "He's out of the D.C. office; his expertise is serial killers." The waitress returned with our food and refilled our drinks. Charley prayed, and then we dug in like hounds. I swallowed a mouthful and said, "Charley, I asked you to lunch for your company, but I had another reason too; a couple of questions about David."

"We're still estranged. I'm working hard to bring us together and improve our relationship. I may not be able to give you many answers."

"How long had David been living with Monica?"

"I believe close to a year," Charley replied.

"That's a surprise; my impression was they had recently met."

"No, that's when I found out about them. The same day I ran into you outside of the police station. David's taking her death hard. Her body is still in the morgue. The Chief Medical Examiner put a hold order on her body."

"Her body can be held until the investigation is closed."

"According to David, she had no family to claim her body. For David's sake, I don't want to see her buried by the county. I'm going to see if I can request the body and give her a Christian funeral. I assumed Sam had killed her too."

"Looks that way, Charley. Did David mention how they met?"

"David worked at a soup kitchen operated by Holy Ghost Parish. I assumed he had given up on his faith and wasn't going to Mass. I spent more time judging him than trying to understand him. That stubbornness cost me a great deal." Charley paused a moment. "Countless times I drove to Knoxville to see him. I believe they met at the soup kitchen."

"During those visits, did you see David and Monica together?"

"Only the one time," he said.

"Don't be too hard on yourself, Charley. Many fathers would have acted the same way."

"That doesn't make it right, Robert."

"Things have a way of working out. Monica Love was an alias for Elaine Keefe, an author. She wrote fiction that centered on corrupt government agencies. A few years back, she dropped out of sight." I pulled out a picture of Keefe and slid it over to Charley. "I copied this from the web." Charley picked the picture up and stared at it. "You see the resemblance?"

"In the picture, her hair is black. She's younger. No mistaking those eyes, though."

"This was copied from the back flap of her last published book. The only book published with her picture on the jacket. Then she dropped out of sight. Charley, you are an avid reader. Have you read any of her stuff?"

"No, but the local writer's guild may be familiar with her work," he said. "Thelma Burke founded the guild. If any member knows anything about Keefe's work, it's Thelma."

"That's good to know." I paused, to give Charley a moment he looked tired and worried. Then I continued,

"Soup kitchens are frequented by people who choose to live off the grid, like Keefe," I said. "I learned that she had a thing for younger men, like your son."

"Like the beggar," Charley said.

"What do you mean?"

"In the Gospel, Robert, the beggar sat at the city gate, calling out, but people walked by him every day and didn't see him."

"They ignored him," I said.

Charley said, "David saw her because he wanted to help people like her. That's why he worked at the soup kitchen, to help people. She took advantage of his kind nature. That's how she got close to him, and he fell in love."

"Do you think she had confided in him and told David her real name?"

"I don't know," Charley replied.

"When you looked at the picture, you said her eyes were unmistakable. She had plastic surgery around her eyes when she became Monica Love. Yet you still recognized her. What if, someone who knew and admired her work could have discovered her identity?"

"I don't follow, Robert."

"I'm thinking out loud, Charley. Whoever killed Keefe had to know her movements where she went and who she kept company with." The look on Charley's face said he understood. "It's probably nothing, but I hope David didn't see that person or give that person a reason to believe he could identify them."

"David knew Sam and Sam's dead."

"The problem is what motivated Sam to kill Keefe?"

"You don't know his motive to kill Todd, either," Charley said.

"Hopefully, the FBI gives us that answer at the meeting. There are still too many unanswered questions, Charley. Stay in touch with David; try to get more information without telling him what we discussed."

"Sure," Charley said and reached for the bill.

"I'll pick up the tab."

Chapter 49

I drove Laura's Beetle out to Sam's farm for Jon's briefing. The FBI had spent a week combing through the house, barn, and the cemetery. Sam was looking like the killer of the century. I parked the Beetle beside Laura's Jeep and walked toward the house. The FBI forensic team was still on the scene. I stopped and looked out across the pasture field to the apple orchard cemetery. Mounds of dirt piled high in different locations gave it the appearance of an archaeological dig.

"Good afternoon, Bob." Jon greeted me when I stepped through the kitchen doorway.

"Hi Jon, how's it going?"

"How's Charley?" Laura asked.

"He's doing well; his son is not doing so well, though." I started to tell Laura the details when Jon interrupted.

"We're almost ready to give the briefing," Jon said. "We're waiting for one more individual. I have scaled back the size of our evidence team to one supervisory agent and four techs. They will stay another day or so. I believe we have found all of the bodies—"

The kitchen door opened and a tall, slender woman, dressed in a dark business suit, entered. Her presence commanded attention. Laura leaned over and whispered, "Sam's mother."

A muscular young man accompanied her. "Looks like she hired her bodyguard from the secret service," I whispered. "The family resemblance was apparent by her demeanor."

"Bodyguard and it's been rumored, lover," Laura alleged.

Jon gave us a look to be quiet and broke the ice. "Judge Reynolds, glad you could make it."

"Your evidence better be solid, Agent." Her voice carried the authority of her position.

Jon cleared his throat, "If everyone will follow me to the living room where our operations center is set up, I will brief you on what we have so far."

I paused at the cellar door. The incident, at Darrell's house, flashed back into my memory. Laura looked at the door too, and we shared a knowing glance.

The living room was spacious. An old-fashioned wallpaper print gave the place a bordello appearance. A large fireplace in the north wall supported a hand carved wood mantle; a scene of the Smokey Mountains. Furniture was stacked at the opposite end of the room to accommodate the large conference table and the bulletin board panels. Against the back wall, a small table held a Buddha idol and an incense pot.

Jon directed us to chairs around the conference table, and he began the briefing. "We believe all of the graves, in the cemetery on this farm, are non-family members. We're still collecting DNA to substantiate it. The total number of bodies recovered to date is sixty. We still have several graves to open. The old style headstones gave the cemetery the appearance it was a family burial ground. In fact, the graves were filled with Sam's victims." Jon pointed to several pictures pinned on the panel. "These are photos of the victims' bones. We have skeleton remains that date back more than twenty years. The most recent body was three months old. We identified her; she was a student at Georgia Tech University. We notified her parents. We're collecting an abundance of data. The graves were dug deep, and that prevented wildlife from destroying the evidence." Jon took a drink of water then continued.

"We are still analyzing, but we have completed analysis on about three-fourths of the bodies found. I can't share identities today; however, the victims are both male and female, varying in ages from eighteen to twenty. All are around the same height and build." Jon continued talking about DNA matching, dental workups, and other forensic matters when I zoned out.

My interest moved to the map on another panel. There were no pins on Tennessee, but surrounding states had markers, with Georgia having the most. The FBI had determined the areas where Reynolds snatched his victims. Laura was taking notes. Reynolds' mother sat rigid and grim-faced, and her bodyguard stood behind her with his hands clasped in front. The guy had to be former Secret Service.

Jon held up a small glass container and identified it as sandalwood paste. Jon said, "It's used in some religions to mark the dead. On Marilyn and Keefe's autopsy report, the coroner found sandalwood paste on their foreheads. We believe they were Sam Reynolds' most recent victims." He paused then added, "Even though they don't fit the same profile of his other victims."

Sam's mother broke her silence, "Is this paste all you have to connect my son to these two women, agent?"

"The method used to kill Todd and Love is consistent with the technique used to kill the victims found buried on this farm," Jon said. "Also, all of the victims' remains, that we have completed examining had markings on their wrist bones consistent with being hoisted up by a chain." Jon paused and then continued, "Technicians recovered a chain and electric hoist from the kill room in the barn. We recovered a similar apparatus in a kill room at the Lancaster home. The Lancaster property had been purchased by Sam Reynolds after Darrell Lancaster's death." I raised my hand, Jon acknowledged me.

"Were all of the victims found on Sam's farm killed in the dugout under the pig stall?"

"That's what the blood work proves." Sam's mother turned on me with a grim expression.

"We have a team working the Lancaster property. So far they have not found any graves, but the cellar had the same setup, and the blood on the dirt floor is human blood," Jon said.

Sam's mother looked back to Jon. "Are you finished, Agent Pate?"

"Yes Ma'am, that's all we can say for now. Thank you for coming, and you're all reminded not to share this information with the press or anyone outside of the local law enforcement. As of now, the FBI will handle the press briefings and brief other departments on a need to know basis. Sam's mother stood and left the room with her bodyguard moving fast to keep up.

"A woman of few words," I said to Laura.

Jon walked up. "Bob, I invited her at your request. I'll be frank. Having the killer's mother present had to be the most uncomfortable situation in a long time. I don't see what it accomplished."

"She's not an emotional woman," I said. "I don't believe she's surprised by anything you reported, Jon."

"I'm surprised she showed up," Jon said.

"Robert," Laura said, "I agree with Jon. What is the connection other than she is Sam's mother? She's a state judge. You cannot believe she was involved with these murders?"

"Being a state judge doesn't give her a free pass, and I don't believe she has a physical involvement, but Sam didn't wake up one day and decided to be a serial killer. There has to be a history of mental illness or something. What do you know about his father?"

"Nothing. Sam never spoke of him," Laura said. "I still don't see the point. Sam lured you to the cabin, and he tried to kill you by running you off the road."

"Laura, I know but we think Sam killed Marilyn, Elaine, and Dew. Yet they don't fit the profile of the victims found on this farm. Why did he deviate? Furthermore, Cree said Elaine saw two people in Todd's house."

"Lancaster didn't fit the profile either," Laura, reminded me.

"That's survival. He had Sam backed up against the wall."

"So, what are you getting at?"

"I'm not sure yet, Laura but something about this doesn't sit right with me."

"I left something out of the briefing," Jon said. He pulled a book out of his briefcase with a gloved hand and held it up. "This is a diary. More than a diary, it's a journal on how to kill and get away with it. We found this in Sam's bedroom nightstand. This journal started with Kane Lyle." Jon watched our expressions as he continued, "I withheld this little book of horrors until Judge Reynolds left."

"Kane Lyle had been murdered in his sleep along with his brother and his father, in 1930," I said.

"This journal says otherwise. Kane killed his dad, and he killed his brother, and an orphan boy." We listened to Jon as he read the account from the journal. He said, "In those days relatives and friends of the family would have identified the bodies by clothing, body shape, and height. The victims' faces were unrecognizable, beaten to the point no one could make a facial identification. There is another passage where Kane described how he found the boy who matched his age, hair color, and weight, his body type. He dressed the boy in his clothes."

Jon looked at us as if our surprised expressions were waiting for the punch line of a joke.

"Why did you withhold this from Sam's mom?" Laura said.

"To be honest, I had to research the Lyle murders. I didn't know very much about the family. I know a lot more after digging through this journal." Jon held the journal up again and wiggled his wrist, "Kane Lyle fled to Nashville. He worked as a day laborer, and by night, he hunted his prey. His victims were women who were petite and lonely. He wrote extensively on how to select, abduct, and murder without leaving a trace of evidence. That was easier to do back in his day. The FBI started their forensic lab in 1932. The science was rudimentary compared to our expertise today. Despite that fact, Sam wrote his own section on how to manipulate crime scenes. He favored abduction and brought his victims to the kill room. There he had time to torture them before he smashed their heads. Sam followed the same path as Kane, who patterned his kills after his grandfather."

"Timothy Lyle?" Laura was stunned.

"Journal books have passed through the Lyle family for years. Kane refers to Timothy's journal. In it, Timothy apparently described his kills and how the curse drove him to savor the evil deeds." Jon paused.

"The founder of Winfield Creek was a serial killer?" I clarified.

Laura followed with, "Sam is a Lyle?"

Jon said, "Sam's mother's real last name was Lyle. She changed it to Reynolds before she entered law school. Sam documented it in this book. He does not explain how he found out about her name change. The journal discovered in the attic had belonged to his late grandfather. I am not sure if Judge Reynolds was aware of the journal or that her father was a cold-blooded murderer. But it seemed like a good reason to have changed her name."

"Kane Lyle is Sam's grandfather." Laura said.

"Yes, and from Sam's journal entries we know Sam killed his father. He wrote about the Cain curse and how it drove his hunger to kill," Jon said. A chill ran up my spine.

"The curse isn't real," Laura said.

"These people made it real, Laura," I said.

"We didn't find the murder weapon in the barn. In the journal, the weapon has a name, Stone Hammer," Jon said.

"Sam believed he had the Cain curse." Laura mumbled, "He seemed rational and sane."

"Serial killers, like Ted Bundy for example, can appear to be rationale they are experts at deception," Jon said.

"Bob, you believed Judge Reynolds was aware of her son's behavior, and that he killed his father?" Jon inquired.

"I don't know, but she separated herself from the Lyle family tree—even the Lyle family pseudonym. Sam had her chosen last name, not his father's or the Lyle name."

"In the journal, he referred to himself as the bastard son. Judge Reynolds did not marry Sam's father."

"Someone has to talk to her, Jon."

"That would be me, Bob. You and Laura stay clear of this one. The political fallout will go nuclear."

"One good thing, Sam is not married," Laura said.

"It doesn't mean he didn't father children," Jon said. "They all wrote about maintaining a future legacy."

Chapter 50

When we left the farm, Laura headed to the office to get some files, and then she would join me at my place for dinner. I turned towards home when my cell rang.

"Mr. Snow, Thelma Burke here."

"Hello Thelma. To what do I owe the pleasure of your call?"

"You're a gentleman, Mr. Snow, and now that you're name has been cleared, please drop over for tea. I have some information to share with you about Elaine Keefe."

"Go ahead, I'm listening."

"Not over the phone. Come to the house."

"Is this information tied to the Todd murder?"

"Indeed, it is," Thelma said.

"Alright, I'm about twenty minutes away."

"Good, I will put tea on, and by the way, come alone." Thelma hung up.

I was surprised Thelma Burke called me. I had received the clear indication she did not like me. After all, she led a group of residents to the Mayor's office demanding my arrest. With the revelation about Reynolds, Thelma may have wanted to apologize for her rush to judgment.

"Good evening Mr. Snow." *This should be interesting*: I thought and stepped into the foyer of her spacious Victorian home.

"Please remove your shoes and place them in the shoe box, there by the door," Thelma said. I did what she asked, and we walked to her dining room. The plush carpet felt like cotton against the soles of my feet, and a mix of oil paintings and chalk drawings hung on the walls. Every piece of furniture looked like an antique. Thelma picked up a silver teapot and poured two cups. She put a drop of honey in each cup with a sprinkle of something.

"A drop of honey and a pinch of ginger, that's my secret," she said. I took the cup and sipped the warm tea.

"Delicious, thank you, you have a beautiful home, Mrs. Burke."

"Thank you, and call me Thelma. I believe we got off on the wrong foot. I just knew you had killed Marilyn, Mr. Snow."

"Thelma, you called me. You have information about Elaine Keefe that couldn't be discussed on the phone."

"Right to the point, I like that about you. What I don't like is your uppity attitude, Bob." I was surprised at her sudden change in tone. I took another sip of the delicious tea.

I said, "I had a successful career as a Special Agent in CID." *Why did I say that*? *What was wrong with me*? I couldn't think straight.

"You didn't like Sammy from the first time you met him. In fact, you had it in for Sammy. That's why you hunted him, Bob." Thelma's face contorted. She leaned over to take the teacup from my hand. *Why didn't she drink her tea*? My mind was numb. My arms and legs were like dumbbells.

"Mr. Snow, you look pale. Let me help you. I have a place where you can lie down. You have overworked yourself. All of this running around town investigating right after your accident has taken a toll on your body. I can help you. I'm a nurse and an author. I know how to take care of people, Bob."

Thelma leaned over me with her hot breath breathing on my face. Her eyes were wide and wild. My mind—fuzzy—like a dream, *what is this old bat doing*? *Is she going to kiss me*? She ran her finger across my forehead.

"Your head is spinning, Bobby. You do not mind if I call you Bobby. Does not matter if you do, I am running the show now. I can smell the whore, Laura Bright, on you. You two have been having too much fun. Tonight, Bobby, you belong to me. I know you are trying hard to fathom what is happening to you. The tea contained my particular recipe. It relaxed your tense muscles.

"An Army wife lives all over the world you know." Thelma droned on in a contorted whisper. "You would be surprised how much clout a General's wife has. A hunter taught the student how to employ enough poison to weaken the muscles of his prey but not kill it. The hunter kills the prey."

Thelma's voice turned raspy and sounded far away. "I taught Sammy everything Daddy taught me. I know. People say we're cursed. We're gifted." My arms were lead.

"Remember, over the phone, I told you I have information for you. Well, here it is, Bobby. There has never been just one." She hovered over me with a wide, vicious grin. "You killed my dearest Sammy, and you will pay."

Thelma moved, her steps made a crackling sound, and I struggled to follow her with my eyes. She came back. I heard another crackling sound. What was it? She looked at me with a wide grin.

Her hand pushed a mask over my face. "This will help, Bobby. I will not let you die from asphyxiation. I have a special plan for you." She removed the mask and held up a large stone on a wooden handle. "This is the infamous murder weapon of the Lyle clan, Stone Hammer," she said. "It's been in the family for centuries. This hammer has eradicated thousands of scum from the earth; you're next, Bobby," she whispered in my ear.

"No Thelma, this ends tonight," another woman's voice warned. The voice was familiar. I had heard it before. Thelma looked away from me towards the door.

"He killed Sammy. He has to pay," Thelma said. Quick as a cat, she moved around the bed toward the voice, screaming. "Sammy carried on the family legacy. I instructed him and nurtured his destiny. You never lifted a finger to help him. Your career was the one thing you cared about, Sister. Sammy did you a favor when he killed your no good husband."

"I know, Thelma. Silence is my crime, but you are not going to kill this man. Sam met his fate. The family killers stop here tonight," the other woman said. Her voice was so familiar. I should remember.

Thelma lunged; their bodies collided against the wall with grunts and high-pitched squeals. I was helpless. I could hardly breathe. My chest—tight, Thelma had the hammer! The two bodies banged against the wall, locked in life and death struggle. Then silence.

Thelma's clawed face hovered over mine. Blood trickled over her lips staining her teeth. Her tongue lapped the blood. My heart sank. She raised the hammer. "This is it, Bobby. This is how you end."

Everything moved in slow motion. My mind could not focus. Then Charley's voice slipped into the confusion. "'When your life is on the line pray: Oh my Jesus, forgive us our sins, lead all souls—'"

A loud bang pierced the air. Thelma fell backward, her eyes wide, and the hammer fell from her hands. She disappeared. I heard a thud when the hammer hit the floor and another thump when her body hit.

Cell phone keys beeped. "We need an ambulance. There has been a shooting."

Calm came over me when the face of the other woman hovered over mine, Sam's mother. Her eye was swollen, her face scratched. She had a fat lip.

She said, "Mr. Snow, help is on the way." She replaced the mask, and air swooshed into my lungs. I drifted—

Chapter 51

When I woke up, Laura was holding my hand, "Hey you."

"Nice to see you standing over me," I said.

She smiled, but her eyes revealed fear. "Do you remember what happened?"

"Bits and pieces. It's like looking at an old picture album trying to identify the people," I chuckled. "I feel like a Mack truck ran over me."

"That was the last time you were in the hospital," Laura said. "You almost bought the farm, this time, Robert. I thought I had lost you. By the way, they found Sam's dump truck in a garage he had rented. The snowplow was attached."

"I'm a tough old codger."

"You do need to actually retire," she said.

"No, I have my private license now. How long have I been in the hospital this time?" I asked.

"Three days. The FBI is still searching Thelma's house. Judge Reynolds saved your life. She and Thelma are sisters," Laura paused. "Sam was Thelma's nephew and her student. She gave Sam the journal after he killed his father. Thelma began to hone Sam's skills. She killed some of the victims buried on the farm while training Sam. Thelma had been at this for a very long time. Married to a military man, she may have victims scattered around the globe," Laura said.

"She never got caught," I said.

"She's caught now. By appearances, she was a righteous woman. Who would have thought she was a serial killer?"

"And Judge Reynolds?" I inquired.

"Jon interviewed her. Judge Martha Reynolds suspected Sam had killed his father, but she remained quiet. She needed that man out of her life. When Jon talked about the bodies in the briefing, Judge Reynolds saw the thread that connected her sister, Thelma. Thelma's novels depicted the same type of methods used on Sam's victims. She had her bodyguard drive her to Thelma's house to confront her when she discovered you were about to be the next corpse."

"What happened to the bodyguard when the Judge had to fight for her life?"

"In the car," Laura said.

"I remember the hammer in Thelma's hand. I could not move to defend myself. Then the gun shot."

"Judge Reynolds used your gun. Thelma had laid it on a side table by the door when she took you to the bedroom."

"Is Thelma dead?"

"No, Judge Reynolds is a bad shot. She gave her sister a shoulder wound. Thelma and Sam shared the kill room at the farm, and the FBI's theory is that Sam used Thelma's poison recipe to control his victims. Thelma got desperate when we killed Sam."

"I had my suspicions about Thelma until Reynolds threw us down the cellar stairs," I said.

"Turned out your instincts were correct. I still can't wrap my mind around Thelma and Sam, serial killers," Laura said. She leaned over and kissed me. "I'm glad Judge Reynolds set aside her career ambition and went to her sister's house. Otherwise, you would be in the morgue instead of the hospital."

"You would miss me," I said.

"I would miss your cooking," she quipped.

"Every time Thelma moved she made the strangest crackling sound," I said.

"Plastic. She covered the floor around the bed with plastic, and she wore paper coveralls."

"You look too healthy to be in that bed, Bob. When do you get out?" Jon said walking into the room.

"In the morning—thanks for coming by, Jon."

"Back to D.C. this afternoon, the local office will tie up the loose ends, and that will take about six months."

"Why did they kill Marilyn Todd and Elaine Keefe, alias Monica Love?" I asked.

"The Knoxville Police searched the Fifth Avenue apartment, where Keefe and the Farber kid shacked up. They found a partial manuscript, Keefe's new book about Thelma Burke, the hidden serial killer.

"She had not pieced together Sam's involvement, at least nothing in her notes pointed to that fact. Keefe was watching Burke, and I suspect Thelma recognized Keefe and figured out why she was followed. Thelma had Sam kill Keefe and dumped her body in your house. It was an attempt to solidify the case of murder against you."

"How did you know she had Sam do it?"

"Thelma and Sam killed with the same weapon, but there are differences. Sam was taller and stronger; his blows made deeper impact impressions on the skull. Thelma murdered Todd."

"Why?" I said.

"She fit the profile Thelma liked. That's all we can say about Todd."

"We had information that Marilyn Todd was an alias too," I said.

"You both know she had worked for the government. All I can tell you is any information on Todd is above my security clearance. However, we did solve another murder." Jon looked at his watch, "I'll make this quick and then have to run. You already know Sam's grandfather, Kane Lyle, wrote his confession in his journal."

"Thomas Lyle murders a cold case is solved," I said.

Jon said, "Yeah, and Keefe was researching Thelma Burke."

"Keefe talked Cree into letting her break in to retrieve the hard drive. Only she did not have time to recover it because the killers surprised her. Keefe ran, and Mason Dew saw her and called the police. Keefe lied to Cree when she said she couldn't describe the second person," I said.

"She knew it was Thelma," Laura added.

"If Cree had known what Keefe was up to, he might have made her stop," I said.

"I'm not sure he could," Jon said. "A woman who made a living at snooping through the government's dirty laundry was not one who would take orders from an assassin. Where do you think Cree went?"

"Not sure—I will find him—bringing Jack Cree to justice will fulfill my promise to John Colbert's widow. When I'm healed, I need to go to San Francisco to see her."

"I will go with you," Laura said.

"Are you sure you can get away?"

"I'm not going to lose you. I've fallen in love." Laura's face glowed. I thought *I'm not going to let her slip away*.

"I love you, Laura Bright." We searched each other's eyes for a long moment. Jon left the room.

Then Laura asked, "What comes next?"

"We will explore the possibilities together. Right now, I'm tired." I closed my eyes; Laura pressed a kiss on my forehead.

"Sweet dreams, Robert Snow, P.I."

Thank you for reading my book. If you enjoyed it, please take a moment to write a review, and recommend my book to your friends.

Follow me on Twitter @sylerma, or M.E. Syler at Facebook Groups.

M. E. Syler lives with his wife in East Tennessee. He is a U.S. Army Veteran, a former police officer in Baltimore, Maryland, and the Veterans Administration. He holds degrees in law Enforcement and Urban Studies with an emphasis in Public Administration.

Made in the USA
Charleston, SC
28 July 2016